Coward's Carnage

From his earliest days Lyndon Barnes had been a coward
and his weak nature had never been displayed to more
effect than when, having been spared by a Confederate
sergeant, he shot the man in the back.

Treachery and murder became a feature of Lyndon's
life as he struggled to set up a new identity. But the time
would come when his past was revealed.

Now he must pay the price but would he finally have
the courage to face his Maker?

Coward's Carnage

BILLY HALL

A Black Horse Western

ROBERT HALE · LONDON

ISBN 0 7090 6962 6

Robert Hale Limited
Clerkenwell House
Clerkenwell Green
London EC1R 0HT

Typeset by
Derek Doyle & Associates, Liverpool.
Printed and bound in Great Britain by
Antony Rowe Limited, Wiltshire

1
Playground Peril

'You're crazy, Barney! You can't beat Spud. Whad'ya wanta play keepers for?'

Lyndon Barnes shifted his eyes back and forth from Binky to Spud. 'Sure I kin,' he blustered. 'I bin practicin'. I'm pertneart as good's Andy.'

Several boys at once laughed and called out playground insults. Lyndon flushed red, but kept his eyes down.

The circle of boys became more raucous. The mood of the whole group had been growing steadily more boisterous as Lyndon Barnes – Barney as he was known to the rest of the kids – and Spud Whitaker were locked in their after-school game of marbles.

'You ain't never beat Spud yet, how's come you think you can today?'

'Your pa finds out you're playin' keepers, he's gonna tan your hide.'

'Go home, Barney, you ain't nothin' but hot air nohow.'

'Do it, Spud. Take all o' Barnyard's marbles. Serve 'im right.'

' 'Member the last time you played keepers, Barney? You lost 'most your whole bag o' marbles. Then you hadta tell your ol' man ya fell down an' dropped 'em in the street an' ol' man Watkins' wagon runned over 'em ta keep 'im from whalin' ya good.'

A chorus of laughter at Lyndon's expense rippled around the circle of boys.

Spud appeared not to hear any of it. He just kept eyeing the large shooter marble in his hand. The iridescent colors caught the sun in ways that still nearly took his breath away. His father had brought it back from a trip to Richmond as a present for him. It was the most beautiful marble he had ever seen in his life. It was the perfect shooter. He had won nearly every game of marbles he'd played with it, except with Andy Bannister.

Andy was, everybody knew, the champion marble-player in the whole school. Even with that ugly mottled-brown, dull shooter he always used, he was all but unbeatable. But with his new taw, Spud had actually beaten Andy once.

'I just cain't bet my shooter,' he said quietly. 'I'll play keepers if'n ya want, but I cain't play keepers with this'n. It's the one my pa got me.'

Lyndon smiled smugly. 'What'sa matter? Yella?'

Spud flushed. 'I ain't yella! I'll play keepers fer the whole bag, any way ya want. Jist not with my shooter.'

'I don't wanta play fer the whole bag,' Lyndon insisted. 'I wanta play fer the shooter. One shot. You kin put it anywhere in the circle ya want. I'll shoot from my mark right here. If'n I hit your shooter, I git it. If'n you hit mine, you git my best agate. This'n right here.'

As he said it, he held out a colorfully marked shooter. It was clearly not as outstanding as Spud's shooter, but was probably better than any other shooter in the school. Spud still hesitated. 'Naw, I dunno. Naw, I jist don't wanta play keepers with this un.'

'You're yella!' Lyndon jeered. 'Spanky's right. You're jist plumb yella.'

'I ain't yella!'

'Are too. A yella Spud's a rotten spud! Yella, yella yella.'

Spud's eyes darted around the circle of school mates. Face red, fists clenched at his sides, he shuffled his feet. He could feel the rest of the boys staring at him expectantly. He took a deep breath. 'All right, Barney,' he conceded, 'but if'n you cheat I'll pound your face clear through the back o' your head, ya hear?'

'I ain't gonna cheat.'

'I'm warnin' ya. Ya better not. How we figurin' who shoots first?'

'We could flip a coin.'

'I ain't got a coin.'

Lyndon looked around the circle. 'Anybody got a coin?'

A long silence followed. Finally Spanky stepped forward. 'I got a Injun-head penny.'

'Flip it,' Spud instructed him. 'Heads, I go first. Tails, Barney goes first.'

Spanky flipped the copper coin into the air. It landed almost in the center of the circle scratched out on the ground. 'Heads,' Spud said. The word exploded from his mouth as a rush of relief. 'I git first shot.'

'Then I git ta put mine where I want it,' Lyndon replied, 'an' you gotta stay on your mark.'

Across the circle from Spud's mark was a small hump in the ground. Lyndon placed his taw there, just behind the hump, so Spud's shot would have to be both long and precise, with enough speed and momentum to keep it from veering off course as it broke over the top of that hump.

'Hey!' Spud protested, 'That's not fair! That ain't a fair shot from my mark.'

'That's the rules,' Lyndon reminded him. 'I kin put mine wherever I want to.'

Spud glowered at the agate and Lyndon in turn. With no further argument to offer, he hunkered over his shooter. He lined up the shot carefully, and fired the iridescent shooter from his thumb. It rolled straight and true until it encountered the hump of ground, then it veered slightly, barely missing Lyndon's agate.

'Ha!' Lyndon exulted. 'Now it's my turn. Put your marble where you want it.'

Spud's forehead furrowed deeply. He brushed a hand through his reddish hair. He looked at the circle. Finally he picked a spot as far from Lyndon's mark as he could, behind the biggest irregularity in the ground he could see.

The circle of boys hovered a little closer to watch

Lyndon's shot. He put his hand to his mark and aimed carefully. The whole group held their breath as one. The silence was intense. Into the silence Lyndon's voice boomed unnaturally loud.

'Now I'm gonna git you!'

The instant he said it, a loud bang sounded from a short distance away. Everyone jumped. Eyes swung to the source of what sounded like a gunshot less than thirty feet away.

Ralph Kitterman grinned at the group. 'Them boards sound almost like a shot when you step on one an' then let it drop agin the other,' he said.

At the sound of the report, every eye jerked away from the circle. In that instant, while all eyes were averted, Lyndon reached across the circle and shot his agate. Spud whipped his eyes back just in time to see Lyndon's agate strike his precious taw. His jaw dropped.

One by one the eyes of the other boys returned. A collective gasp arose as they realized Lyndon's shot had flown true to the mark. All eyes riveted on Spud. Spud swallowed twice. Lyndon reached across and swept up his agate and Spud's shooter.

'It's mine now!' he exulted. 'I won it fair'n square.'

Spanky's quiet voice filled the empty silence. 'Did not,' he asserted. 'You cheated. I didn't look when everyone turned around. You fudged. You reached clear across the circle to shoot when nobody was lookin'. I know. I saw you. I bet you had Ralph make that noise when you said what you did, jist so you could cheat.'

Every eye swung to Lyndon. His mouth was

suddenly dry. His knees wobbled. He looked into the rising fury in Spud's face. He could barely force his voice to work. 'He's lyin',' he protested.

Ignoring the protest, Spud gritted, 'Gimme back my marble, you . . .'

Lyndon thrust the marble back at Spud. 'Here! Take it! I don't want it nohow! I was jist funnin' ya.'

Spud grabbed the marble and lifted the closed fist of his other hand. 'I said I'd pound your face through the back o' your head if'n you cheated,' he yelled.

A squeal much like a horse pursued by a cougar would make emitted from Lyndon's mouth. He broke and ran, with Spud in hot pursuit, followed by the crowd of boys yelling and shouting. Lyndon ran in blind panic. He flew across busy streets, narrowly escaping being trampled by horses and wagons. Riders and teamsters yelled and cursed at him as they swerved, then fought to control their frightened animals.

Lyndon heard none of it. He no longer knew if Spud was hot on his heels or left far behind. He could hear nothing except the pounding of his heart and the blood rushing in his ears. His chest felt as if it would explode. He didn't hear the sobs and squeals emanating from his mouth. He felt nothing except an overwhelming, all-consuming, fear. The unbearable panic knew no respite until he was home, huddled on the floor in a corner of his bedroom, gasping for breath. Only then did he realize he had wet his pants.

2

Cowardly Triumph

'Lyndon! I want to talk with you.'

Lyndon cringed at the anger in his father's voice. His steps dragged as he walked into the house.

'Why, Lyndon,' his mother said, 'you're soaking wet. Where on earth have you been?'

'I, uh, went over after school an' took a dip in the big tank at the livery stable. Us kids like to swim in there sometimes, you know.'

'But, in your clothes?'

'Aw, gee, Ma. We can't go skinny dippin' in town!'

Lyndon's father interrupted. 'Lyndon, I've just had a very disturbing visit from Ephraim Whitaker. He seems to think there was some sort of problem between you and Samuel.'

Lyndon swallowed hard. 'Uh, no. Not really. We was jist playin' marbles.'

'Were you playing keepers, Lyndon?'

'Uh, well, sorta, I guess.'

11

'What have I told you about playing keepers? That's gambling, as far as I'm concerned, and we do not gamble in this house. But that's not the thing that disturbs me the most.'

Lyndon waited silently. After what seemed like a very long time, his father continued, 'Ephraim tells me that you cheated to try to take that marble he bought for Samuel in Richmond.'

'Spanky tol' 'im I cheated, but I didn't cheat, Pa. Honest.'

Lowell Barnes glared at his son. 'Lyndon, tell me the truth, or it will go twice as hard on you. I will not have a cheater for a son. The three things I cannot tolerate are a liar, a cheat, and a coward. And if I have to beat you within an inch of your life out there in that woodshed, you will not be a cheat. Now tell me. Did you cheat?'

Lyndon tried twice to swallow the huge lump in his throat. Finally he croaked, 'Yes, Pa. I had it rigged up to have Ralph slap a couple boards together when I said I'm gonna win, so's I could fudge a little when nobody was lookin'. Only Spanky, he was watchin'.'

The session in the woodshed that followed might not have been as severe if his clothes hadn't been so wet. Being wet, the pants clung to his skin and amplified the sharp sting of every blow of the wide board. Even so, it was preferable to admitting he had wet his pants, and went for that swim only to rinse them out and hide the evidence of his cowardice.

As his father spanked, Lyndon sobbed and screamed and begged, until his father finally said in utter exasperation, 'I don't know why you can't even take a paddling like a man. The neighbors will think I'm some kind of monster!'

That description fitted Lyndon's opinion precisely. Not only was his father a monster, but so was Ephraim Whitaker. But most of all, Spud Whitaker was a monster. He was a monster that had to be dealt with. If it was the last thing he ever did, he promised himself, he would deal with Spud Whitaker.

Day after day, at school and after school, Lyndon watched Spud. He played out fantasies in his mind, in which he faced Spud and beat him to a quivering pulp for squealing. He beat him for being bigger and stronger. He beat him for owning that wonderful, magnificent marble, that Lyndon had only held in his hand for that one brief moment. He beat him for being brave. He beat him for all the things he, Lyndon, was not. But only in his mind. In reality, he kept his distance and tried his best to keep Spud from noticing him at all.

It was nearly a month before the chance came.

Opportunity reared its head the day Fred Blessmer brought one of his bulls into town. He brought it in restrained with two ropes. Fred and his hired hand mounted on strong horses, each had one of the ropes tied to his saddle horn. They walked the huge bull, hobbling along on three feet, through town and corralled it in the strongest corral behind the livery barn. Fred went directly to the blacksmith shop.

'Hey, Charlie,' he greeted the blacksmith. 'How are you?'

'Fit enough,' Charlie Macomb, the blacksmith, responded. 'What's on your mind, Fred?'

'Big ol' bull o' mine's ailin',' Fred answered. 'Wondered if'n you could take a look at 'im.'

'What's 'is problem?'

'Got a front foot he can't put no weight on. I cain't see nothin' wrong with it, but it's sure enough sore. I cain't afford fer him to be too lame to breed my cows.'

'That the big mean one?'

'That's him. Meaner'n thunder, but jist about the best bull I ever had. Works night 'n day, long's I got a cow in heat. Ain't had no more'n one er two cows stay open since I got 'im.'

'Well, we'll take a look.'

Charlie picked half a dozen ropes off of pegs on the wall and walked with Fred to the livery barn.

When they arrived at the livery barn, a group of the boys who had just gotten out of school had already gathered. Word of a mean bull being brought into town had spread like wildfire on a windy day, and they were quickly caught up in the excitement.

From the corral fence, Charlie looked at the bull for a long moment. 'Looks like he's got somethin' stuck in that foot,' he observed.

'Yup,' Fred agreed. 'Now all we gotta do is ask 'im to pick that foot up an' hold real still, an' let us work on it.'

'I'm sure he'd agree to that,' Charlie observed.

He made a loop in one of the ropes and cast it at the bull. As it settled over the animal's head, he dallied it quickly around the base of one of the huge posts that held the rails of the corral. The bull bellowed and pulled against the rope.

Moving quickly, Charlie circled the corral and roped the bull again, tying that rope around the base of a post on the opposite side, holding the bull in the center of the corral, unable to move to either side.

The prison of the two ropes infuriated the bull. He bellowed and pawed, jerking against the ropes until they began to choke him too much to resist.

Calmly ignoring the animal's temper. Charlie walked into the corral and cast a loop that turned over unerringly to capture one hind leg of the animal. That rope he passed up to the animal's head. Staying just where the huge animal could not hook him with what head movement the ropes allowed, he tied the rope around the base of the horns, making it impossible for the bull to kick him with the hind leg.

Then he took a fourth rope and looped it around the lame left front foot. Ignoring the bull's roaring defiance, he hauled the front foot up, looped the rope across the animal's neck, and secured it to the base of the horns as well.

Tied immobile, one foot off the ground and one hind foot imprisoned by the encircling rope, the animal was helpless to do more than bellow his anger and slobber profusely.

'Yup,' Charlie said quietly to the bull's owner, standing at his side, 'got a stick o' some sort wedged atween the sides o' his hoof here.'

Taking a pair of tongs, he grasped the offending piece of wood and pried it out. The bull's bellowing changed from rage to pain as he fought vainly against his tethers.

With the piece of wood extracted, Charlie poured kerosene over the bottom of the foot. 'That'd oughta do it. You'd best keep 'im here a few days, though, to make sure that foot don't fester up. In a week er so, he'd oughta be as fit an' good natured as ever.'

Working quickly, Charlie removed the rope from the injured foot. Then he removed the rope from the hind feet. He moved to the side of the corral and untied one of the ropes holding the bull's head. The bull rolled his eyes and pawed the ground. Moving quickly but carefully, Charlie walked to the huge animal and grabbed the loop passing around the bull's neck. He jerked it off, as the bull strained against the other rope, trying to reach the blacksmith.

As Charlie backed away, the bull suddenly realized it was free to move toward the spot where the other rope was tied. He trotted a couple steps that way, then wheeled back toward the blacksmith.

Sensing what was about to happen, Charlie started to run. Bellowing his frustration and rage, the bull charged. When he hit the end of the rope that was still tethered, its loop still around his neck, the rope snapped like a thread.

The bull thundered after the fleeing blacksmith. As Charlie leaped for the corral fence, hands reached out to grab him and lift him over. Snorting and huffing, the bull tossed his head and trotted around the corral, pawing the ground, slobbering and glaring his defiance.

'Looks better already,' Charlie observed.

'Movin' on it a heap better,' Fred agreed.

Charlie and Fred started to leave. As they did, Fred turned back to the group of boys perched on the top rail of the fence.

'You boys better git down from there an' go on home now. If one o' you falls into that corral, that ol' bull'd kill ya sure.'

He watched to see that the boys were starting to climb down, then he turned and followed the blacksmith away. In groups of two or three, the rest of the boys drifted away, but not before tossing stones at the bull and yelling taunts at him, just to watch him paw the ground and run at them.

Standing back in the shadows of the livery barn, Lyndon could hardly believe his good fortune. The rest of the boys were gone. Nobody was in sight. Spud alone was left, perched on the top rail of the corral, quietly tossing stones at the bull, grinning at his futile wrath. His back was turned squarely toward Lyndon.

Moving swiftly and silently, he hurried to the corral right behind Spud. He watched the bull. As the animal trotted toward his lone tormentor, Lyndon stepped up on to the bottom rail of the corral, put both hands on Spud's rear as it hung over the fence, and shoved as hard as he could.

Caught completely by surprise, Spud was too startled even to yell as he was propelled from the top rail directly into the path of the oncoming bull. Any opportunity to yell for help ended abruptly as the ground drove his breath from him. Before he could struggle to his feet, the huge animal's horns hooked him, tossing him into the air. When he landed, the bull was on him in an instant, driving with nearly a ton of weight, ramming his broad head down into the soft body, then hooking him to toss him into the air again. As he hit, the bull stomped on him, trying with all four feet to drive him into the dirt, then turned and hooked him, shoving his limp body across the corral and back.

As soon as the bull hooked the hapless boy the first time, while he was still flailing helplessly in the air, Lyndon faded back into the shadows at the back of the livery stable. Keeping close to the wall, he sidled around away from the corral, and made his way up the alley, coming out close to the street he lived on. He stepped out into the street and walked along, back toward the livery stable, swinging a small stick at pebbles in the road, as if he hadn't a care in the world. He hummed softly, smiling to himself as he walked along.

Back at the livery stable, the hostler glanced out the back door, then stopped and yelled. 'Hey! There's somebody out there! Thet bull's got somebody down!'

He ran to the front door of the livery stable and yelled into the street. 'Hey! I need some help! Fred's bull's got somebody down!'

Grabbing a pitchfork, he ran out into the corral. Half a dozen men were right behind him, responding to his yell. Three of them had grabbed pitchforks as they ran through the livery stable. Jabbing the bull in his tender nose, they forced him, slobbering and snorting, away from the limp body in the dirt. As they held him at bay, a man grabbed up the boy and ran through the livery barn into the street.

The men backed slowly out of the corral and shut the gate, then joined the growing crowd around the lifeless body of Spud Whitaker.

At the fringes of the circle, Lyndon Barnes watched silently. A small smile played across his mouth from time to time. Aside from that, he showed no emotion.

3

The Worries of War

Dust hovered everywhere.

'How kin it be this dusty when the air's this heavy?' Beau complained.

Lyndon shook his head. He coughed the particles of dust from his throat as he swatted a mosquito on his neck. 'Beats me,' he concurred. 'You could wring enough water outa the air to water this whole army, an' it's still too dusty to breathe.'

'Skeeters is bad, too.'

'Bigger'n hummin' birds.'

'Don't 'member 'em bein' this big 'round home.'

'Too fur north. Up here they fly over ta Washington once in a while. Feed on thet blue Yankee blood. Makes 'em big an' mean an' stupid.'

Beau chuckled. Both men devoted themselves to keeping up with their units, marching in silence for nearly a mile.

Swarms of gnats hovered in front of their faces.

Sweat ran down into their eyes, forcing them to mop their foreheads frequently. The yells and curses of the mule-skinners seemed to be the only conversation for a while, as they pushed and prodded their mules, hauling along the heavy pieces of artillery.

Finally, after what seemed an eternity, orders were shouted to fall out for a brief rest. The yells of the mule-skinners continued as they fought to keep up with the swifter marching infantry.

Beau and Lyndon, acting as if on some unheard command, immediately grabbed their canteens and took a long drink.

Wiping his mouth with the back of his hand, Beau said, 'How's come ya reckon Bee pulled us off 'n the stone bridge?'

'Figgered it's a diversion,' Lyndon guessed. 'They wasn't enough Yankees a-comin' to be a real attack. He figgers the Yanks is gonna send their real outfit at us upstream, somewheres.'

'Was you up front, back there?'

'Where? Stone bridge? Naw. I only jus' got here yistiday. I was a-headin' thataway when they called us back an' had us form up to march. Was you?'

'Yup. Got me my first Yankee, I did. Put my sights right on his breastbone an' squeezed it off. He throwed up 'is hands an' fell flat on 'is back. Never moved a muscle.'

'How'd it feel?'

'Oh, it felt good! I was plumb scared afore thet. I wasn't noways sure I could really shoot a man, thataway. I was plumb scared I'd cut an' run er somethin'. Soon's I plugged him, the fear done ran outa

me like water runnin' outa a leaky bucket. I jist
plumb felt like a man, I tell ya.'

Lyndon started to answer, but the command to fall
in carried down the long line of soldiers. They
heaved to their feet and fell to marching in silence
once again.

By mid afternoon they were stationed and waiting.
The officers had selected a spot just south of a farm-
ers' ford across the Bull River. A line of Confederate
troops dug in facing the river. Artillery pieces were
set up and ready behind them.

'Who's the rich guy?' Beau asked, nodding toward
their right.

Lyndon looked where he indicated. An older
Confederate soldier, resplendent in the finest
uniform and accoutrements, was being tended by a
young slave. Lyndon chuckled. 'Would ya lookit thet!
Brung 'is boy with 'im! Wonder how the boy feels
'bout helpin' 'is master fight a war to keep 'im a
slave?'

'Hadn't thought o' thet,' Beau pondered. 'I was
jist thinkin' how nice it'd be to have one. I seen 'em
all set up down by the stone bridge. They was jist a
little ways from me when the Yankees sent that bunch
at us, ta feel us out. "Fetch me a drink, boy. Load my
rifle, boy. Wipe this sweat offa me, boy. Load this rifle
agin whilst I shoot t'other un at them Yankees, boy."
Did you notice he's got two rifles, Barney?'

Lyndon nodded. 'Yup.'

'That's what he was doing at the bridge. He'd be
aimin' an' shootin' whilst his boy was a-loadin' the
other'n. That nigger can flat load a rifle faster'n

anyone I ever seen. Ever' time the guy'd shoot, thet boy'd have 'is other rifle loaded an' ready.'

The young black man looked up at them as Beau made the observation. Because neither Beau nor Lyndon were paying attention to him, they failed to notice the small smile Beau's words of praise brought to his lips.

'Git ready! Here they come!' was whispered urgently and passed along the line.

Lyndon rolled over and peered across the fallen tree behind which he and Beau waited. He checked the cap on the nipple of his rifle. He swallowed hard. He started to say something, but found his mouth suddenly too dry to speak.

As if on some signal he failed to hear, rifles started barking on all sides. Immediately, the artillery behind them erupted in a deafening roar. It was answered instantly by artillery from across the river. A great crashing roar ripped through the trees over and around them. Leaves showered down like snow falling, accompanied by the crashing of larger limbs and twigs.

A wave of blue uniforms surged across the river toward their position. Federal troops, yelling and running toward them, fired impossible numbers of volleys at them. To his right, Lyndon saw the owner of the young black man calmly and methodically aiming and firing, exchanging rifles with his slave, aiming and firing. He acted as if he were target practicing on some fine plantation.

At his side, Beau was loading and firing as rapidly as possible. He was so intent on the battle he failed to notice Lyndon had yet to fire his rifle at all.

Lyndon's hands were sweating so profusely he could scarcely hold the rifle. He thrust it across the fallen tree and looked over its barrel at the charging blue line. As he did, the Yankee soldier at whom he aimed looked straight into his eyes. A sob tore its way through Lyndon's clenched lips. Just then half the Yankee soldier's face was torn away by a 50 caliber rifle ball.

'Got 'im,' the gentleman soldier said softly, reaching for a reloaded rifle.

Lyndon rolled away from the tree and hurriedly reloaded his own rifle, unaware he had not yet fired it. Powder, wad, ball. Old cap off. New cap on the nipple. He rolled back and thrust his rifle across the tree again.

This time he didn't even put his face to the stock of the gun. He looked into the oncoming charge of blue and jerked back again. He reloaded the rifle again.

To his right, the gentleman soldier stood up suddenly. A dazed look of confusion stamped itself across his face. A growing red stain began to spread across the chest of his immaculate uniform. He fell forward, not moving.

After only a brief hesitation, the young slave pulled a piece of paper from his owner's pocket. He scanned it quickly.

'He kin read!' Lyndon breathed.

The black man pocketed the paper, picked up one of the rifles, a bag of ammunition, and moved quickly away from the battle.

Lyndon turned to Beau. The words were already framed in his mouth to ask, 'What was thet thar all about?'

He never got to ask. As he turned to Beau, Beau's left eye suddenly disappeared. A fountain of blood and shattered pieces of flesh and bone erupted from the back of his head. He sagged against the fallen tree, held in place by dead branches. His right eye stared sightlessly at Lyndon.

Lyndon screamed. He stood up and threw his rifle to the ground. He no longer heard the deafening noise of battle. He no longer saw the trees above him being ripped to splintered shards. He saw only the faces of the charging army of Brigadier General Irvin McDowell. He screamed again.

Turning from the battlefield, Lyndon ran headlong. He left the cover of the trees along the river. He fled through the line of artillery. He ran past the horses and mules and supply wagons.

Faintly, as he left, he heard the command to fall back, and the unit he had been with began to retreat toward Henry Hill. He did not slow his steps.

Blood pounded in his ears. He gasped for air. Suddenly he spotted a sergeant, mounted on a fine bay gelding, barring his way. The sergeant dismounted, directly in his path. He grabbed him by the shoulders.

'Hold up there, son,' the sergeant said.

Lyndon stopped. His chest heaved. His knees quivered. His eyes, too wide open, cast about wildly. 'Jist hold up a minute, son,' the sergeant repeated. His voice was slow and steady, as if he had just settled into a rocking chair on his front porch. 'Jist give yerself a minnit. First taste o' combat, huh?'

Lyndon nodded wildly.

The sergeant's grip on his shoulders never slackened. 'Happens thetaway,' he said. 'Most young fellers sorta panic, the first time they gotta watch folks gittin' shot up an' all. Jist give yerself a minnit. Take a coupla deep breaths. Your courage'll come back ta ya, straight away. Then ya kin mosey back over an' rejoin your outfit.'

Growing sounds behind him forced Lyndon to turn and look. As he did, the sergeant's grip on his shoulders loosened. General Barnard Bee, astride his horse, galloped along the ragged line of fleeing Confederate soldiers. Standing in his stirrups, brandishing his sword, he pointed toward a line of dug-in Confederate troops. 'Look!' he called to his troops, 'There is Jackson standing like a stone wall! Rally behind the Virginians!'

His men looked from him to General Thomas Jackson's troops. They slowed their retreat. The panic left their flight. They veered to positions behind the Virginians.

'Thet's your outfit,' the sergeant told Lyndon. 'You kin rejoin yer outfit right over there, an' nobody'll ever know we chatted here.'

He turned away from Lyndon to remount his horse. As soon as he turned his back, a sudden transformation overcame Lyndon. His breathing slowed. His eyes narrowed. In a swift and smooth motion, he drew the revolver he had forgotten at his belt. With no hesitation or thought, he fired directly into the sergeant's back. The bullet struck him squarely between the shoulder blades, driving him forward, on to his knees.

He turned, looking over his shoulder at Lyndon. 'What did . . . Why did. . . ?'

He never finished either question. He collapsed on to his face, then rolled over on to his side.

With a small smile playing around his mouth, Lyndon stepped across the body and reholstered his gun. He picked up the reins of the sergeant's horse. He swung into the saddle and rode away.

He did not even notice, standing less than fifty yards away, the young black slave. He had no way to know the piece of paper in his pocket was his writ of emancipation, written by his owner to give him his freedom in case he himself was killed in battle.

Even if he had seen him, Lyndon would probably have never really noticed him. Slaves were just there, they were not really noticed, much like a dog or a cow.

That the young slave had seen him would never enter his mind.

4

The Battle and
the Bottle

'Sure never thought it'd go on that long.'

The old sergeant palmed his beer and moved it back and forth on the table in front of him. Four other soldiers lounged around the table.

'Rebs was stubborn all right,' a private agreed.

Along one side of the room a bar was set up. It was little more than planks laid across empty beer barrels, but it served its purpose. Behind it, on planks supported by more barrels, the saloon's stock of beer and liquor stood ready to serve the soldiers of the fledgling Fort Fetterman, and cowboys and occasional sheepmen from the surrounding ranches.

'Just too stupid to know when they were whipped,' the sergeant disagreed.

The influx of both soldiers and settlers following the war found a demand for alcohol that far exceeded the available supply. It didn't take long, however, for entrepreneurs to set up shop in any kind of shelter they could erect to try to quench the insatiable Wyoming thirst.

'Some o' them boys at Bull Run were the bravest soldiers I ever saw,' the private argued. 'If they wasn't as gutsy as they was, they'da kept on runnin' when we pushed 'em back. It was just pure guts that they rallied behind Jackson an' drove us back instead.'

The five new arrivals to Fort Fetterman were lost in reminiscing about the war. There was word whispered now and then that Confederate soldiers had been mustered into the Federal army, but nobody particularly cared, so long as they didn't have to serve with them. If there were any former Confederates in the present group, they certainly were not making the fact known. The nation was united again, more or less, but feelings still ran high.

Those who remained in the South became permanently embittered at their treatment at the hands of the carpetbaggers. Many of them left land no longer theirs and headed west. Much of the problem for Wyoming grew from the fact that many of the cowboys, the homesteaders, and even some of the ranchers, were Southern refugees or sympathizers, while the military was nearly all Federal.

'Not the ones I seen,' the sergeant challenged.

Lyndon Barnes sat alone at a grimy table, pretending not to hear. He could feel the eyes of the sergeant continually boring into him, however.

'Fact is,' the sergeant continued, staring at Barnes, I seen one Johnny Reb there at Bull Run that was about the yellowest varmint I ever saw. He was all set up where he could've dealt us fits. Hunkered down behind a tree, he was. Couldn't get a clear shot at 'im, no matter what we did. Trouble was, he was too yellow to shoot his gun. I could see him from where I was pinned down. I watched him load his gun two or three times, and never even shoot it.'

Lyndon did his best to ignore him, downing his beer and making his way to the planks that passed for a bar for a refill. Instead of returning to the table, he picked out an empty spot further from the table of soldiers. His gait was slightly unsteady as he moved around the table and fell into the chair.

He took a big drink of his beer and set it down. He glanced out of the corner of his eye at the table of soldiers. The big sergeant's eyes were still fixed on him. He jerked his eyes back to his beer.

The sergeant spoke again, more loudly. As he spoke, his companions finally picked up on the direction of his conversation. They began to watch Lyndon.

'Fact is,' the sergeant said, 'I could see half a dozen Johnny Rebs behind that same tree. Big ol' linden tree, it was, that a storm had just laid down flat. All the roots was still on it, half of 'em stickin' up in the air. Made fine cover.'

He paused and took a drink of his own beer. 'There was one o' them Southern gentlemen, there, that was some kinda man, in spite o' bein' a slaver,' he said. 'He had his colored boy loadin' his rifles, an' he was rackin' up a load o' dead bodies, let me tell ya. I don't think he ever missed. He'd fire a rifle and hand it to his colored boy. The colored boy'd hand him a loaded one and take the empty. He'da pertneart wiped out the whole lot of us before we could get to him, if one of our snipers hadn't got a bead on 'im from a tree. Sniper dropped him, and his colored boy just dropped back and took off.'

'I know him,' a soldier said unexpectedly.

All eyes left Lyndon and swivelled to the speaker. 'You know who?' demanded the sergeant.

'The colored guy.'

'From Bull Run?'

'Yep.'

'You're kiddin' me!'

'Nope. It's a fact. His name's Isaiah Walker.'

'How'd you know that?'

'I know him.'

'From where?'

'The Hasacker place. I rode fer Hasacker several years.'

The sergeant seemed to have trouble collecting his thoughts in this new direction. 'You wasn't in the war?'

'Nope. I was out here in Wyoming. Figgered the war was back East, mostly. I just joined the army last year.'

'An' you know this ... what's his name? The colored guy?'

The soldier nodded. 'Name's Isaiah Walker. He rides for Hasacker too. Good man. He was a slave, afore the war. He had papers his owner had drawed up, what gived him 'is freedom if'n his owner got killed. His owner got killed at Bull Run, he said, so he took the paper an' lit outa there. 'Course he don't need 'em now, since the niggers is all free. He keeps it anyway, though.'

The sergeant pounded the table with his fist. 'There! Didn't I tell ya? Jist like I said it happened. Don't that beat all! All the way out here, an' that nigger boy's workin' on a ranch right out here. I seen that Southern gentleman take the bullet what freed 'im, I did! Now that there is jist what the war was all about. We done freed thousands an' thousands o' them slaves.'

The others nodded sagely. Almost in unison they lifted their beers and drank, as if in a ritual salute to the glory of the war and the freedom it brought to a race of the enslaved.

The sergeant wiped his mouth with the back of his hand. His eyes swung back to Lyndon. 'I'll tell you what else I saw,' he said. 'That there yellow coyote what was too much of a scared little puppy-dog to ever shoot his gun. When his buddy got shot, that Johnny Reb started screamin' like some little girl gettin' raped. He jumped up and throwed his gun on the ground an' lit out runnin' like nobody you ever seen in your life. Last I seen of 'im, he was runnin' an' screamin' an' wavin' 'is arms like a lunatic. He run plumb outa sight.'

The eyes of the soldiers darted back and forth between Lyndon and the sergeant. They laughed nervously, still unsure where the sergeant was going with it.

The sergeant continued, as if without interval. 'Until today.'

He turned in his chair to face Lyndon squarely. 'Until today, he run clear outa sight. But I'll he danged if that fella sittin' right over there doesn't look jist exactly like that yellow Reb I seen runnin' an' screamin' from Bull Run.'

A deathly hush fell on the saloon. All eyes were suddenly fixed on Lyndon. The blood drained from Lyndon's face. He wanted to stand, to run, to get outside, but he wasn't sure his trembling knees would hold him. He looked around at the room full of eyes staring at him. His heart began to pound so hard he thought it would burst the walls of his chest.

He raised a hand. 'You got the wrong man,' he protested. His voice sounded squeaky. 'I wasn't never in the war. Came out from Kentucky ahead of it.'

All eyes in the saloon swung back to the sergeant. As soon as the eyes left him, Lyndon felt a surge of courage. He jerked to his feet. Not looking at the sergeant, he nonetheless stabbed a finger toward him.

'You'd best be sure of your facts before you go tellin' tales on people. A man with a worse temper than what I got might just shoot you fer sayin' somethin' like that.'

He rushed to the door and out into the night. He ducked around the corner of the saloon and back into the empty lots behind it. Away from the sights and sounds, he stopped. He put his hands on his knees and bent forward, gasping for breath. The earth wheeled around him dizzily. He staggered sideways, then caught his balance. He fought to still the hammering of his heart.

Suddenly he retched violently. The contents of his stomach spewed into the grass and weeds. He hauled in great gulps of air. He spat the foul tasting residue from his mouth.

Straightening, he wiped his mouth with the back of his hand. He stared stupidly in the darkness at the smear he couldn't see across his hand. He walked a couple paces away and bent down to wipe his hand on the grass. He toppled over and fell.

He rolled over on to his back and lay where he was, looking up at the night sky. Innumerable stars stared back at him, turning slowly and silently as if they were all drunk. He sighed heavily. He rolled over on to his stomach and pulled his knees beneath him. From that position he wiped his hand on the grass until it felt clean. Then he hauled himself to his feet. He staggered a little, but kept his feet.

'Stupid idiot!' he fumed. 'Who's he think 'e is, comin' clear out here tellin' everyone what 'e thinks 'e saw back there. Shoulda kept 'is mouth shut, that's what 'e shoulda done. It ain't Lyndon Barnes he's dealin' with now. Nossir. It's Lang Hart, now. An' Lang Hart ain't gonna stand for that sorta stuff. Lang Hart ain't afeered o' nobody. 'Specially some drunk ol' soldier. Lang Hart knows where your horse is, tough soldier. Jist wait'll you try ta head back to the fort, that's what. You'll see.'

He staggered off toward the livery barn.

Nearly three hours passed before the group of soldiers left the saloon. They were laughing and yelling boisterously.

'Hey, Sarge,' one of them chided. 'You shoulda left your horse here like the rest of us done. Then you wouldn't have to go clear to the livery barn to get 'im.'

The sergeant shook his head. The slur of his words

betrayed the amount of beer he had drunk.

'I treat my horse better'n that, Private,' he said. 'I'll saddle up an' beat you to the fort by half an hour, an' my horse'll be fresh when I get there. You boys'd best learn to treat your horses better, too. That horse is all that'll keep the Injuns from liftin' your scalp, one day. If he's fresh an' strong, you'll live to run away another day.'

'Hey, the Johnny Reb done that,' another soldier called. 'He lived to run away!'

The laughter of the others followed the sergeant as he staggered into the livery barn. A single lantern hung from a peg, offering only scant light to the interior. All of the stalls except the one right by the lantern were shadowed in darkness.

In spite of his drunken state, the sergeant moved quietly and easily to his horse's stall. Muttering softly to the animal, he backed him out of the stall, into the alleyway. He saddled and bridled him. Just as he finished, he thought he heard a noise. He paused and turned.

'Someone there?' he asked softly.

There was no answer, no sound. He listened intently for a long moment. He watched his horse, but the animal showed no sign of alarm. Shrugging, he turned and reached for the saddle horn. Just as he did, a hard blow clubbed down on him from behind. Fierce, hot pain stabbed through his back, clear into his chest. He stumbled forward against the saddle. The horse snorted and backed away.

The sergeant whirled to see what had struck him. A shadowy figure stood in the alleyway. The lantern at the end of the alleyway glinted off the blade of a large knife. The sergeant balled his fist and started to swing at the shadow. The forward motion of his arm threw him off balance. He tried to catch himself but couldn't. He pitched forward, catching himself on his hands and knees.

He struggled to regain his feet. He tipped his head back to look at his assailant. 'Who? What?' he gasped.

His breath and bright blood gushed out between his lips and he plunged forward. His face landed squarely in the dirt of the alleyway. He made no effort to turn it sideways so he could breathe. He had no more need for breath.

'Teach ya to run off your big mouth,' the shadowy figure muttered.

Moving through the darkness, the shadowy form went out the back door of the livery barn. He stepped into the saddle of the waiting horse and set off at a trot.

5
Meander Creek Refuge

Lang Hart, once known as Lyndon Barnes, gazed across the mountain valley. He hooked his leg around the saddle horn, sitting almost sideways in the saddle.

'That's gotta be the most beautiful spot on earth,' he breathed.

The grass between his horse's legs stood tall, swaying in the gentle breeze. To his left, Meander Creek babbled across the rocks, sparkling in the spring sunshine. Brush along the creek gave way on the west to clumps of aspen trees. Above and beyond the aspen groves, pine and spruce timber painted shades of green, interspersed with expanses of grassland. To the east the grass was spotted with sagebrush, but almost without trees.

Behind the timber to the west, the mountains stood as silent sentinels to protect the awesome beauty of the land. Their shades of blue and purple, streaks of brown rock and black shale, extended to peaks hidden beneath many feet of snow. The white-capped beauty seemed to touch the impossibly brilliant blue of the sky.

As Lang watched, a lone eagle floated effortlessly on some invisible shaft of rising air, seeming to be almost motionless in the clear air.

A splash brought his eyes back to the creek, too late to see the cutthroat trout that had leaped for an insect, then disappeared beneath the swift current of the stream. His eyes fell on a mule deer stag, standing across the creek, watching him with calm appraisal. He seemed without fear, standing stock still, like a perfect statue. Then, abruptly, his tail shot up in a signal of immediate danger. He wheeled and bounded gracefully away, looking for all the world as if his legs contained some kind of hidden springs.

Lang sighed heavily. 'Right there, the house goes,' he said. 'Where I kin sit on the front porch an' watch all that beauty till my heart jist plumb busts.'

He had found the site less than a week earlier, then hurried to file his homestead on it, as if someone might beat him to it if he waited even one more day. Now the vision of a ranch stretching clear to the mountains filled his mind.

'Ain't gonna be one o' them tar-paper shacks or dugouts,' he told his horse with firm conviction. 'I'm gonna build a real log house. I kin rig ropes so's the team kin hoist the logs, and I kin do 'er all by myself.'

He remembered those words many times. If he had known the amount of work he had committed himself to doing, he might well have settled for a shack instead. But Lang Hart was not afraid of hard work. He spent most of the money he had on supplies, a team and wagon, and the bare minimum of equipment to begin a homestead. Then he began the arduous labor of chopping trees from the timber, well away from his home site, cleaning the branches from the great logs, then dragging them by team to the site of his house-to-be.

When he had assembled what he thought would be enough logs, carefully chosen for similarity of size and shape, he began to build the house. He dug into the rocky soil as much as he could, to build a foundation. Then he hauled and carried flat rocks to build that foundation nearly two feet above ground level. On that foundation he laid the square of logs that would start the outer walls.

At the spot where he wanted the front door, he labored for two back-breaking days to dig deep enough to stand vertical logs into the ground on either side of the door. Then he hewed the ends of all the other logs to mesh together on the corners, fitting the logs as tightly together as he could.

In the middle of the wall opposite the door he built a huge stone fireplace. Its chimney angled upward into a spire that reached well above where the roof would be. In front of it he laid a stone hearth that would keep sparks that flew from its fire from reaching combustible materials.

The back wall of the house reached from both sides of the fireplace to the corners, then forward to the front corners, then toward each other until they encountered the timbers set into the ground for the door.

He worked from the first rays of the sun to the last glimmer of daylight, day after day, week after week. He worked silently, alone, fuelled by his dream. Sometime during the heat of summer he sweated away the shame of his cowardice and the chagrin of the mocking words that had spurred him to violence. His muscles grew and swelled and bulged. He began to whistle as he worked some days. As the log cabin took shape, his sense of belonging and contentment began to grow.

Somewhere in the exhausted blur of those labors the precious hoard of whiskey he had brought with him became less important. He resorted to it less and less, until he realized with a start he hadn't touched it for a month.

From cedars that grew a few miles to the west he hewed shales for the roof. His skill with axe and adze grew until they looked almost professional.

When the roof was finished he made mud and chinked between the logs, inside and out, sealing them against air, moisture, and tiny or slithering intruders.

Inside he laid more logs for a wooden floor, adzing the tops of the logs flat. Then he hauled a wagonload of cut boards from a sawmill and made a wooden floor on top of the logs. He fitted the board carefully to the hearth in front of the fireplace, allowing not even space enough for a snake to crawl up from beneath into the house.

He used more of the boards to make a wooden

door, fitting it carefully into the jamb of timbers sunk into the ground. The windows he covered with oiled paper, promising himself to replace it with real glass as soon as he was able.

When the house was finished he looked at it with pride akin to gazing on a beloved child. 'I knowed I could do it,' he exulted.

The shelter for his horses was far less carefully made, and took little time. He built a corral on either side of it, then began putting up enough hay to get them through the winter. He was beginning to run short on both food and funds, but he knew winter wasn't that far away. He already had all the supplies he needed to set up a trap line for the winter, and he was confident it would provide.

Long before snow flew, he had ricked up great piles of wood from the branches he had cleaned from the logs and from dead timber he had cut. Enough wood was stored within easy carrying distance of the door to heat the house for three winters.

Only then did he realize he would need a place to store the furs he intended to trap until spring, when he could sell them. Working almost frantically he built another shed beside what passed for a horse barn. He sealed it tightly, knowing rodents would ruin his pelts if he did not. It never even occurred to him that he was giving far more consideration to the safety of his pelts than to the comfort of his horses. Mostly, when he wan't using them, he simply hobbled them and left them free to seek their own grass and water. He only checked them occasionally to be sure the hobbles weren't making sores on their legs.

When winter settled in, he began to work the trap line. When the snows piled up too deeply to wade, he made himself snowshoes. The winter was long and cold, so the pelts became thick and rich. He could almost count the money they would fetch in the spring.

It wasn't until nearly spring he began to feel lonely. The long hours of darkness began to weigh heavily on him. Dreams began to bring back the horrors of war. He returned to his cache of whiskey, nursing it carefully lest it fail to last until spring.

When spring finally broke, he could scarcely contain himself long enough to let the thawing ground firm. As soon as he had any hope of making it all the way to town with a heavily loaded wagon, he carefully stacked and piled his winter's wealth of furs on to the wagon. He spent most of one day catching the team and bringing them back into a semblance of working attitudes.

Just before the sun bathed the verdant land the next morning, he hitched the team and settled into the seat. The wheels of the wagon bit deeply into the soft ground, but the horses managed to pull it well enough; he thought they would last the distance to town. If not, he would simply camp for a night and make the trip in two days rather than one.

Almost four miles downstream he topped a low rise and jerked the team to a stop. At the edge of a meadow, in a spot of pristine beauty nearly as perfect as his own homestead, a large tent was pitched. A makeshift livestock shelter had been erected. One corral was almost finished. Dirt had been dug from a square that was obviously intended to be the location of a house.

Someone else had homesteaded along Meander Creek!

Lang felt a rising tide of anger well up within him. Then he laughed at himself. Of course other people would homestead along here! That's why he had filed his own homestead so urgently and worked it so diligently. He still had the best spot available. Neighbors wouldn't be a bad thing at all.

All at once the loneliness that he had felt through the last couple months of winter swept over him. He wanted to shout, wave his arms, run down the hill and hug these strangers he hadn't even seen yet.

On the heels of the urge, a tide of terror filled him. Who were they? Would they be friendly? How would they respond to him? Would it be someone who would try to steal his furs?

He sat there, frozen to the seat, too lonely to stay, too frightened to move.

As he sat there, a young woman stepped out the door of the tent and started toward the creek, carrying a bucket. She glanced up and spotted Lang sitting on the top of the hill. For just an instant she froze in her tracks. He could see her say something toward the tent, but he was too far away to hear.

Almost at once a man stepped from the tent. He held a rifle loosely in his hand. He gazed steadily at Lang. After the briefest of hesitations, he lifted a hand and waved to Lang. His wife followed his lead and began to wave excitedly, as though she were suddenly delighted to see another human being. Across the distance the man's voice carried faintly. 'Come on down. We're just fixin' breakfast.'

Lang's breath, that he hadn't realized he was holding, exploded through his lips. He lifted a hand in response and clucked to his team. He slapped them several times with the reins to hurry them. It seemed to take far too long to reach the family's encampment.

By the time he pulled up beside their tent, the man and his wife were standing together, grinning at him. 'Boy, you're a sight for sore eyes,' the man exclaimed. 'We ain't seen nobody 'cept each other since the big snow. You'd be Lang Hart?'

Lang climbed down the wheel of the wagon and gripped the man's extended hand. 'That's right. I got the homestead up the crick.'

'I'm Ralph Hopper,' the man responded. 'This here's my, wife. Freda.'

Freda held out her own hand, gripping and shaking Lang's enthusiastically. The thought flashed through Lang's mind that if he had something as breath-taking as Freda Hopper to look at every day, he wouldn't care if anyone else ever came by.

He forced his mind back to the conversation. 'You folks homestead this?'

'Yup,' Ralph responded. 'We only just had time to set up somethin' for the animals an' pitch our tent last Fall. Winter was somethin', let me tell ya, livin' in that there tent. Four times the snow got too heavy on it an' pushed it down on us.'

'We like to froze to death gettin' dressed so we

could shovel the snow off and get it fixed up again,' Freda giggled.

For the first time Lang noticed the bulge of her stomach. She noticed the drift of his eyes and blushed prettily. 'We're gonna have a baby this summer, too,' she boasted. 'Ain't this just the most perfect place in the world to raise a family?'

'Most beautiftil spot I ever saw in my life,' Lang agreed. 'You got to get a house built afore that baby comes, though. You can't be havin' a baby in a tent like some Injun.'

Ralph scraped his foot back and forth on the ground uncomfortably. 'Yeah, we're fixin' to start on that right away,' he said. 'Ain't sure how good I can get it done afore she's due, but I'll have to give it my best shot, I guess.'

Lang hesitated a long moment. Thoughts tumbled over each other in his mind. He couldn't keep his eyes, or mind, from the face and the body of Freda Hopper. An ache from deep within him prompted feelings he had never experienced before.

'Well,' he said, 'I got to get these here furs into town an get 'em sold. I built my own house last year. Fine log house, if I do say so. Did it myself. If'n you was to want me to, I 'spect I could sorta come down an' help you build one here. I learnt a whole lot a-doin' mine. I 'spect two of us could build one twice as fast.'

It took several heartbeats for Ralph to respond. 'You'd do that?' he asked.

'Why not?' Lang said, a little too quickly. 'We're fixin' to be neighors, ain't we? Ain't that there what neighbors is fer?'

'Well, that'd sure be a godsend, it would,' Ralph mused. ' 'Course, I ain't got no way to pay you.'

'You don't pay neighbors,' Lang protested. 'I'd be right proud to do it fer the company. Been a long winter.'

'Well, I'll sure take you up on it then. Come on. Let's have a bite of breakfast.'

Over that breakfast Lang decided a one-year wait on his own place wouldn't be that long anyway.

6

Good Neighbours, Good Times

Lang stood in the footrest of the wagon, waving his arm back and forth. Excitement he couldn't suppress telegraphed itself to his team. They pranced and snorted.

In the meadow below, Ralph and Freda Hopper returned his wave with every bit as much enthusiasm as his own.

Lang forced himself to sit down and drive the team. He urged them forward at a trot. As he hauled them to a stop in the Hoppers' yard, he leaped from the seat. The Hoppers crowded around him. Freda laid a hand on his arm, as Ralph gripped his hand. Lang scarcely noticed the enthusiastic welcome of Ralph's grip, however. A sensation from Freda's touch washed through his body, leaving him almost breathless.

'How did you do?' Freda asked.

'Did they sell good?' Ralph echoed.

49

'Better'n I ever even hoped,' Lang exulted. 'I got more'n twice what I was hopin' to git. An' I got at least one more real good season on that trap line afore the numbers dwindle any. I kin buy what I gotta have fer the year, an' then some. I kin spend the whole summer helpin' you folks git your house built, if'n you want.'

Freda's hand tightened on his arm. 'Oh, could you? Oh, that would just be so wonderful, wouldn't it, Ralph?'

Ralph's enthusiasm was even greater than his wife's. 'Boy, howdy!' he breathed. 'You'n me together, we can maybe even get the house roofed afore the baby gets here.'

'Found out somethin' else, too,' Lang enthused.

'What?' both Hoppers asked at once.

'Three miles on down the crick is another homestead. Fella with a wife an' four kids. His wife's been a midwife, back in Ohio. She says when it's pertneart time fer the baby, she kin come up here an' jist stay till it comes, to help out an' all.'

'Oh! Oh, that's just, that's just beyond words,' Freda responded. 'That's the only thing I've really worried about, and only three miles away! Oh, Ralph, you could even go get her after I start, if she isn't here yet, and have plenty time. Oh, that's just so wonderful! Oh, Lang, already I don't know what we'd do without you. You are a godsend, that's what you are.'

'A plumb godsend,' Ralph echoed.

Lang looked slightly awkward for a moment. 'Uh, I done somethin' else too. If'n you folks don't mind, I went an' bought myself a tent, too, whilst I was in town. I figgered if we was workin' on your house sun-up to sundown, it'd take quite a bit o' workin' time away if'n I was ridin' clear up home every night an' back every mornin'. If you don't mind, I thought maybe I could jist pitch my tent over there, a ways away from you-all's, an' jist sorta camp out here most o' the time.'

'Makes sense to me,' Ralph agreed.

'Oh, I think it's just a wonderful idea,' Freda agreed.

Almost at once Lang and Ralph fell into a routine working together. Ralph had a huge team of mules that worked steadily and well. With Lang's team of horses working with them, they felled, cleaned, and snaked logs down from the timber in less time than Lang would have thought possible. Freda took care of the stock, had their meals fixed when they were ready to eat, and allowed them to spend their entire time and effort building the log house.

With a level of audaciousness that took even himself aback, Lang said, 'Hey, Ralph. Let's not jist build a one-room cabin. Let's build a three-room house. We kin build the fireplace so's it's in the wall and faces out into two rooms, an' if the third room is the kitchen, it'll heat with the range. Then we could put in a loft without too much trouble, an' you'd have a house that'd be plumb perfect fer a family fer years ta come.'

Ralph stared at him. 'I wouldn't even know how to do that! I wouldn't know how to support the roof or nothin', for a house that size.'

'We kin do it,' Lang assured him. 'I was thinkin' about it the whole time I was buildin' mine. You seen my house?'

Ralph nodded. 'Me'n Freda rode up an' looked it over, while you was off to town, sellin' your furs. That's gotta be the best-built log cabin I ever seen!'

'It ain't nothin' like what yours is gonna be,' Lang boasted.

'Why?'

'Why not?'

'Why are you that interested in my house?'

Lang shrugged. 'Why not?' he repeated. 'We're neighbors. I got the know-how. Workin' together, it ain't gonna be that much work. I'll need help with somethin', down the road. You'll have a chance ta get even.'

'I'll sure owe you, that's for sure,' Ralph hesitated. 'Well, if you're sure we can do it, why not?'

The next morning Freda approached him. Ralph was harnessing the mules, well out of earshot. 'Lang, Ralph told me what kind of house you want to build for us. I can't begin to tell you how much that means to me. I grew up in a real house, and the only thing that really bothered me about coming out here to homestead was knowing I'd have to live in some shack. But I don't understand. Why would you want to do that for us? We don't hardly even know you. Yet.'

Lang tried hard to swallow the lump that rose into his throat. He forced himself to keep his eyes averted from hers, as her eyes probed his face. 'I jist think you're worth it, that's all,' he said. He couldn't keep the huskiness from his voice. 'You're the most beautiful woman I ever see'd in my life. I jist can't bear the thought o' you livin' in some shack, er havin' that there baby with no fit house to raise 'im in.'

Her eyes continued to probe his. 'You aren't expecting something in return, are you? From me, I mean?'

Lang felt a sense of panic rise suddenly within him. ' 'Course not!' he said, entirely too emphatically. 'Nothin' like that ever entered my mind! Why, that'd be . . . I mean . . . No! I mean, if'n you wasn't married an' all, I 'spect I'd jist plumb camp on your doorstep, but I ain't noways tryin' to double-cross your husband.'

'Thank you,' she said softly. 'I was sure you weren't that kind of man, but I needed to ask. I like you far too much to think you'd be like that.'

She squeezed his arm affectionately and walked away. He hurried to help Ralph with the mules.

The days that followed became the same blur of exhaustion that had marked the whole of the previous summer. They laid the foundation for the house that was easily three times the size of Lang's own. They hauled the rocks and built the fireplace, with an even larger hearth extending out into each of the two rooms. Lang patiently instructed Ralph in the techniques of using the axe and adze to shape and fit the logs together. With two of them working together, the speed of building was at least tripled.

As they worked, Lang watched Freda working about the tent and the yard. By the time they had the doorposts set for the house's two doors, she was large enough for him to identify her pregnancy whenever the wind blew her dress against her. By the time the walls were erected, her stomach kept a distinct hump in the front of her dress all the time. By the time the roof was on, he began to worry about her being due.

In spite of Ralph's assurances that they had plenty time, he worked feverishly to get the floor put in, and the logs chinked. When they were ready for the sawn boards of the floor, he and Ralph took the wagon to the sawmill to buy them. Because Ralph and Freda didn't have the cash, Lang paid for them himself, assuring Ralph he expected to be paid back as soon as they could.

The day they hung the front door on the house, Freda gave a sudden cry and grabbed her stomach.

'What is it?' Ralph and Lang asked as if with one voice.

'Oh! It hurt!' Freda answered. Her eyes darted from one of them to the other. 'I think it was a pain. It all just kind of cramped up, like.'

'I'll go get Mildred!' Lang said. 'You stay with Freda. Get 'er in the house. Take stuff from the tent. Make her a bed in the house. Don't you go lettin' 'er stay out here.'

Not waiting for an answer, he sprinted to his horse. He saddled and bridled the animal, leaped into the saddle, and left the yard at a dead run.

Freda giggled. 'He's more excited than you are,' she teased Ralph.

Ralph frowned. 'I know. Worries me some.'

'Oh, Ralph! Don't be silly. Oh! Oh, it's another one. I have to sit down! Help me into the house,

Ralph. I want to have it in our new house, not in that dreadful tent.'

Hopelessly inconsiderate even before it was born, the child waited almost twenty-four hours to venture into the world. By that time both Ralph and Lang were nearly frantic, listening to Freda's screams and moans from outside, expelled from her presence, and offered only the occasional assurances from the midwife that everything was just fine.

Lang finally rode to his own place and retrieved a bottle from what was left of his stash. By the time the baby finally arrived, neither man was able to walk a straight line.

They were both allowed to see the baby, a fine strong boy, and to see Freda for only a moment. Ralph held her hand and stared in awe at the infant. When the midwife told him to go, she pulled him down and told him softly, 'I love you, Daddy.'

Eyes suspiciously moist, Ralph plunged out the door. As he turned to go, Freda caught Lang's hand. She pulled him down. 'I love you, too, Lang Hart,' she said softly. 'Thank you for giving me a real house to have my baby in. Don't ever leave.'

Lang wasn't sure whether it was her words or the whiskey that caused the roaring in his head. In the days following, however, he knew it was her words.

Ralph went directly to his tent and collapsed into his bed, falling at once into a drunken stupor. Lang wandered toward what passed for the horse barn. The mules were standing where stalls should have been, halters tied to a long rail. He scooped up a handful of small rocks, pouring them idly from hand to hand.

On impulse, he threw one of the rocks at the nearest mule, striking him in the flank. As the rock hit, the mule kicked with a speed and force that took Lang aback. He stared at the mule for a long moment. Frowning, he took another stone and threw it, striking the animal in the flank again. The mule kicked again, just as hard. Aside from kicking, however, he seemed unaffected. He went right back to munching the hay Ralph had piled in front of them.

Lang chuckled softly, and threw another stone. The mule kicked again, then resumed eating.

Half a dozen stones later, Lang tired of the game. He wandered to his own tent and fell into bed. He fell asleep to fantasies of Freda in his arms, in his life, in his bed.

7
Kicking the Triangle

'Ain't he just the most beautiful baby ever, Lang?'

Lang glanced at the baby and jerked his eyes back instantly to Freda's radiant face. ' 'Course 'e is,' he said softly. 'He's your baby. Any baby o' yours jist naturally has to be beautiful.'

'Oh, Lang,' she responded. 'You say the sweetest things. You do the nicest things, too. How did you ever get real glass for our windows?'

'Had the general store order it. Took 'em three months, but they got it. Came in wooden crates, all packed in sawdust, it did.'

'What would I ever do without you?'

Lang glanced out the window to be sure Ralph hadn't returned. Assured, he turned to Freda. He reached for her and she came into his arms instantly, eagerly. Their lips met greedily.

After several moments, she pulled away. 'Oh, Lang. We have to stop this. I love you so much! But I love Ralph, too. Why can't I just have two husbands?'

' 'Cuz I'd kill 'im,' Lang said simply. 'I wouldn't never share you with nobody. If you wuz mine, I mean.'

'I truly wish I'd married you instead of him,' Freda responded. 'I truly do. You care so much more about me. Ralph just cares about this place, and having that ranch he wants. I'd have had the baby in that tent if it wasn't for you.'

'From the first time I laid eyes on you, I knowed I'd do anything in the world for you,' he answered. 'Buildin' this here house was plumb easy, since I was doin' it for you.'

'Ralph knows.'

'What!'

She laid a hand on his arm. 'Oh, he doesn't *know*. I don't mean that. But I'm sure he knows I love you. He can just sense it, I think. He knows you love me too. He mumbles about it in his sleep, sometimes. I'm so afraid he'll get jealous enough to send you away and not even let you come visit us. Then I wouldn't be able to see you any more. Oh, Lang, I'd just die if that happened.'

'I gotta go,' he said abruptly.

'What? Already? Why? Ralph shouldn't be home for two or three hours yet.'

'I gotta go,' he repeated. 'If he's gettin' suspicious, I don't wanta be hangin' around here in the house when he gets back. I don't want him callin' me out or nothin'.'

'Why, Lang! Are you afraid of Ralph?'

'I ain't afraid o' no man alive!'

'Then what's your hurry? Ralph isn't going to say anything. He wonders, but he trusts me. He trusts your friendship. Even if he's worried, he trusts you not to do anything to destroy your friendship. He knows we'll never actually . . . well, you know.'

'But I want to,' Lang said.

Her eyes were liquid pools with an undertow too strong for him to ever resist. 'I do too,' she said softly. 'I want you so bad I can taste it. I want to hold you, and kiss you, and make love to you till you're so exhausted you can't get out of bed. We just can't. Not now.'

'I gotta go,' Lang said again, glancing out the window.

'Kiss me first.'

She came into his arms again. Without words, her lips made him forget all about Ralph Hopper for a little while. His fear returned, however, pushing him away from her embrace.

'I gotta go,' he whispered.

She ran the tips of her fingers down across the smoothly shaven plane of his jaw. 'Ralph wants you to come over tomorrow.'

'What?'

'Ralph said if you stopped by, to ask you if you could come over tomorrow and help him. He wants to fix that bad corner of the corral by the barn. He said if you weren't too busy getting your stuff ready for the trap line, he could sure use some help.'

'Oh. OK. Tell 'im I'll be here an hour or two after sun-up. I gotta go.'

He rushed out of the door, mounted his horse,

and rode out of the yard at a quick trot.

He tossed and turned most of the night, rising well before dawn. He rode into the Hoppers' yard less than half an hour after sunrise.

Ralph Hopper opened the front door. 'You're up bright an' early,' he greeted his friend. 'Just in time for breakfast. You eat already?'

'No, matter o' fact I didn't,' Lang responded, avoiding Ralph's eyes. 'I was hopin' I could get here in time to eat you folks outa house 'n home.'

Over his shoulder Ralph called, 'Freda! Put another plate on the table. Lang'll eat with us.'

Then to Lang he said, 'Well, come on in. You gotta look how this fireplace works. I lit a fire this mornin', to take the chill off. Look at this!'

He went into the front room, gesturing to the fire burning brightly in the fireplace. The warmth of the fire radiated to every corner of the room, but Lang couldn't pick up any smell of smoke at all. 'Chimney draws just perfect,' Ralph exulted. 'Best fireplace I ever seen.'

Freda stepped up beside Lang. So her husband could not see, she rubbed Lang's back as she spoke. 'It really is. The house is going to be so warm and cozy all winter. I just love this house! Come on, you two. Breakfast is getting cold.'

Lang was aware of nothing through breakfast except Freda's presence at the table. As soon as they were finished, he rushed from the house.

'Plumb anxious to get to work, ain't he,' Ralph mused as he followed.

As Lang tied his horse to the rail in the barn,

Ralph began harnessing the mules. Lang studied him over the top of his saddle for a long moment. When he threw his saddle over one of the three saddle trees he had helped Ralph make, he stooped down and picked up a couple small stones.

'Little cloud bank in the west,' he mentioned. 'Looks like we might be in for a change in the weather.'

'That right?' Ralph responded. 'I didn't even look.'

He stepped around the corner of the barn to study the sky. As soon as he was out of sight, Lang walked over and dropped a ten-dollar gold piece in the dirt of the barn, just behind one of the mules. Then he hurried out to join Ralph.

They discussed the implications of the clouds for a few minutes, then went back into the barn. Lang walked in beside his horse, about ten feet from the nearest mule and watched. His heart was racing. His hands were sweating so hard he could scarcely hold the rocks. Hands shaking, he picked out one stone from the several in his left hand, holding it in his right.

As Ralph walked in to resume harnessing the mules he stopped.

'What's that?'

He bent over to retrieve the coin. As he did, Lang raised his arm to throw the stone. He hesitated. He looked at the smiling face of his friend. He swallowed hard. He lowered his arm. Silently, he shook his head. He dropped the rocks.

Ralph stayed bent over, squinting at the gold

piece. He brushed the dirt from it. Abruptly he whistled sharply. The instant he whistled, the mule
kicked. Its hoof connected with Ralph's head, bent
over behind him, with a sickening thud.

Lang stood frozen in unbelief. A puddle of blood
spread from beside Ralph's head, seeming reluctant
to soak into the trampled dirt. A half-circle depres-
sion marked Ralph's skull, the exact size and shape
of the mule's hoof. Glancing over, he noticed blood
and hair clinging to the edges of that hoof.

He raced around the stall and knelt beside Ralph.
He felt for any breath. He felt for a heartbeat. There
was neither. Grief and exhilaration tumbled over
each other in his mind. The life that stood between
him and the woman of his dreams was gone, like a
candle flame in a sudden wind, and he hadn't even
done it! He removed the ten-dollar gold piece from
Ralph's fingers, dropping it into his pocket. He felt
Ralph's face again, surprised at how rapidly his body
was losing warmth.

He whirled and sprinted to the door of the barn.
Yelling at the top of his voice, he began to run toward
the house. 'Freda! Freda! Come quick! Fredaaa!'

The door to the house opened. Freda emerged,
wiping her hands in her apron. He called to her.
'Freda! Come quick! It's Ralph. The mule done
kicked him.'

'What? Is he OK? Oh, Lang, what happened?' she
cried as she ran.

He waited for her, half-way between house and
barn. 'I dunno what happened,' he said. 'I was takin'
the saddle off my horse an' stuff. I jist heard some-

thin'. Kind of a thud. I looked, an' Ralph was jist layin' there.'

She ran by him, sprinting into the barn. At sight of her husband she stopped. A gasp escaped her lips. She started toward Ralph, but Lang grabbed her. 'Wait a minute. Let me move that mule. I don't want 'im kickin' you too.'

He moved ahead of her and untied the mule from the rail. He moved him a few feet down, on the opposite side of the other mule. By the time he retied him, Freda was on the ground, holding her husband's head in her lap. Tears streamed down her face.

'Oh, Ralph. Oh, Ralph. Oh why did you have to go and get that careless? Oh, Ralph, I'm sorry. It's my fault. I just know it's because of me and Lang this happened. Oh, God, I'm sorry. I'm sorry. Oh, what am I going to do?'

Lang knelt beside her, putting an arm around her shoulders. 'I'm plumb sorry, too, Freda. I sure didn't want it to come to nothin' like this here.'

Freda turned to look into his eyes. Her own were already red and puffy. 'You didn't do this, did you Lang? You didn't do this, so you, so we, so . . .'

'Oh, no, no, Freda. I wouldn't never do nothin' like that. Oh, Freda, how could you think that? It was the mule, Freda. Look here. See. That's the mule's hoof caved his skull plumb in. See. It's the same shape as his hoof. An' look. See the blood an' hair on the mule's hind hoof?'

Her eyes followed the pointing of his finger. The blood and hair clinging to the hoof were clearly visible. She realized there was no way Lang could have made it look as it did, if the mule hadn't, in fact, kicked Ralph in the head.

She sighed heavily, leaning against him. 'Oh, Lang. That's such a relief! For just a minute I was so afraid you had done it. For me. I'm so glad you didn't.'

Lang swallowed hard. 'I love you enough I might've,' he admitted. 'But I couldn't. He was my friend.'

'What will we do with him?'

Lang sighed heavily. 'I 'spect maybe we'd best fix 'im up an' haul 'im down to Carlson's. Have them help us bury 'im. That way they'll see the mule's hoofprint in his head too, so's nobody'll ever think maybe I kilt him to have you.'

'What will we do then?'

'I dunno. Nothin', fer the time bein'. After two, three months, maybe we could, I mean, if you was willin' an' all, maybe, I mean along 'bout then I 'spect I'd be askin' you to marry me.'

She was silent for a long moment, stroking the blood-soaked hair of her dead husband. 'Do we have to wait that long?'

'For what? To get married, you mean?'

'Well, no. I know we'll have to do that. If we get married too quick, people will talk. But I mean, well, do you have to live clear up there at your place alone, while we wait? I really don't want to stay here all by myself. I mean as soon as the neighbors all leave and everything.'

That was a problem for which he knew the perfect solution.

8

Grey Ghosts and Hard Times

'I'll be needing a bit more credit, Mr Steinhaus.'

The general store's owner frowned. 'You're getting in pretty deep, Mr Hart.'

'I've stretched us a little thin, all right,' Lang agreed. 'But we're really in pretty good shape, for the long haul.'

'And what do you base that on, Mr Hart?'

'Well, as you know, Freda has almost a hunnert chickens.'

The storekeeper peered over the top of his glasses at him. 'And they are particularly hard to keep from the coyotes, are they not?'

Lang nodded. He couldn't keep the rueful expression from his face. 'That's why we had to buy so much chicken wire. We had to fence 'em clear in, an' even over the top, to keep the coyotes from eatin' us outa business. But we got it done. We ain't hardly lost a chicken in three er four months.'

'Well, that is good. But it will take a long while for your egg money to pay for all that fencing.'

'But it will,' Lang insisted. 'And there's the milk.'

Steinhaus nodded. 'You are one of the very few in the country with milk to sell. That is a possibility of some profit. But with only four milk cows, and you have to let them dry up before their next calf is due . . .'

'But it all helps,' Lang insisted. 'And Freda is a real hand at raisin' them vegetables.'

'She is a fine gardener,' the store-owner agreed. 'And a hard worker. Such a tragedy about her husband. It was good you were there for her, or she would have lost that homestead before she really got started. You are keeping your own homestead as well, I am told?'

Lang nodded. 'We're provin' up on both of 'em. Got a good house on mine too. Just not as big as our house on her claim. We're raisin' oats too, you know.'

'I had heard you were ploughing up some of the ground and raising some oats. They should make a crop along the creek, I would think.'

'They're lookin' good, and oats is at a premium. Horses need oats, an' it costs so much to freight 'em, we'll be able to get quite a bit o' cash outa that crop.'

'And what of your cattle?'

Land grimaced. 'We don't have near as many as we need yet. Jist ain't had the money to get the herd started yet. But it'll come.'

'Why do you say that?'

Lang hesitated. He needed these supplies. He owed the storekeeper nearly two hundred dollars already, and more than sixty dollars' worth of supplies were stacked together. If he didn't bring the supplies home, Freda would be very difficult.

He had never understood how Freda could be two such different people. When things were going well, when she got what she wanted, she was the warmest, most loving wife he could ever have imagined. There were times he wondered if he had died and gone to heaven. The baby was walking, and she was considering whether it was time to stop nursing him. He really wanted her to do that. He hated sharing her. At the same time he knew as soon as she stopped nursing the baby, she would probably get pregnant again They really couldn't afford another child just yet. Besides, then there would be another baby to share Freda with.

Then, at other times, when she didn't get what she wanted, she could be as cold as a block of midwinter ice. She could instantly turn spiteful, demanding and mean. She ranted at him, accusing him of murdering her husband, threatening to have him hung. He was truly afraid of her when she was in one of those moods, and stayed away from home until he thought her mood might have changed.

If he came home today without these supplies, he knew what to expect.

'I, ah, don't really want to say too much,' he hesitated, 'but I did get a letter a while back.'

Steinhaus's eyebrows raised inquisitively. He said nothing, waiting.

Lang continued. 'I have some family back East. Some of them are pretty well off. A kin died recently, and I guess I'll be gittin' a share of thet inheritance. The letter was from one o' them lawyers what's dealing with it.'

Steinhaus's eyebrows went up another notch. 'Ah, that's good news, eh? Where is this family?'

'Uh, South Carolina.'

'Ah, yes.'

Just then the bell attached to the door tinkled. A black cowboy walked into the store. He went to the shelves along one wall and began selecting some items.

'Who's the nigger?' Lang asked the storekeeper.

'Ah, yes. His name, I believe, is Isaiah Walker. He is one of the hands on the HD ranch. Slim Hasacker, you know. He has been with Slim since the war.'

'Is that right?'

'Fine hand, I'm told. Quite a story, too.'

'Oh, really?'

'Yes. It seems he was a slave, belonging to one Beauregard Walker. Was his personal boy. When Beauregard enlisted in the Confederate army, he took his slave with him. Used him to load his rifles. Carried three fine rifles with him, so he could keep up a rather steady stream of fire. Acquitted himself very well in battle, I'm told, until a mini ball took him right in the heart. He died instantly. On his person he had papers granting his slave freedom in the case of his death. According to the story, Isaiah verified that his master was dead, calmly removed the papers from his pocket, took a rifle and pistol and his master's horse, and rode from the field of battle a free man. Came West and hired on with Slim Hasacker.'

Lang knew his face had gone ashen. He stuttered

when he spoke, despite his best efforts to sound casual. 'Wh . . . wh . . . what outfit was this Walker in?'

'Bee's army, I believe. It was the first battle at Bull Run. Early on in the war.'

Scenes of the battle paraded unbidden through Lang's mind. He smelled again the dust and blood and sweat and horses and gunpowder-smoke on the wind. He smelled again his own raw, naked fear. He heard the screams of the wounded and the dying. He heard the battle yells of the charging Yankees and the answering yells from the Confederate lines. He saw, as if he were there, the Southern gentleman repeatedly and calmly firing into the lines of attacking Yankees.

He saw the young black man turn and look at him as he and his friend discussed him.

He looked across the store and saw the same eyes calmly staring into his own. He felt the blood drain from his whole body, leaving him lifeless and cold, standing utterly exposed. He strained with all his might to keep from wetting his pants.

With no indication of recognition, the black man turned back to assembling the supplies he was selecting.

When the black man turned his back, Lang instantly relaxed. The tension drained from him. His attention whipped back to the storekeeper. He felt the sweat on his forehead. He wanted to wipe it off, but didn't want to call attention to it.

'I really got to get to headin' back out home,' he said. 'We'll be payin' up the whole bill afore long, though.'

After a moment's hesitation, Steinhaus said, 'Very well. This really will have to be the last credit I can extend, though, until you bring the arrears up to date.'

'Sure thing,' Lang assured him. 'Much obliged.'

He gathered the things he had selected and hurried out, making three trips to load them into the wagon he had driven into town.

9
Opportunity Calls

Lang Hart slapped the team and pulled away from the front of the general store. His mouth was drawn into a thin line. Didn't think thet two-bit junk-peddler was even gonna give me the stuff, he fumed softly. Freda'd been fit ta be tied if'n I'd'a come home without it.

He looked over the row of horses tied up in front of the saloon. The smell of beer and sawdust drifted on the breeze. A woman's surprised squeal, followed by a cowboy's laugh, floated from the open door.

Lang pulled the team to a stop. He sat there for a long moment, licking his lips. He pulled a watch from his vest pocket and studied it. 'Aw, I 'spect I got time fer a quick drink afore I head home,' he muttered.

He pulled the wagon over to the side of the street. Wrapping the lines around the brake, he climbed down the wheel and shuffled over to the bar. He stopped just inside the door to let his eyes accustom to the dim interior.

As soon as his eyes adjusted, he sauntered to the bar. 'Whiskey,' he drawled to the bartender.

The bartender set a shot of whiskey before him, took his money, and gave him change. Lang dropped the change into his pocket and tossed off the drink. He stood there, holding the shot-glass, feeling the warm glow of the whiskey course down his throat and spread across his stomach.

He held up the shot-glass to the bartender, who immediately refilled it and took the money.

Lang picked up the shot-glass and made his way to an empty table near the wall. He sat down with his back to the wall and studied the patrons of the saloon. A few soldiers clustered near the front door. Two of the saloon's 'working girls' chatted with them, flirting and laughing.

Four men stood at the bar. Two of them faced the bar, lost in their own thoughts. The other two stood with their backs to the bar, boots hooked on the brass rail, elbows on the bar, watching and visiting with others in the saloon.

Nearest to Lang, four men sat talking animatedly. He ignored them, lost in his own thoughts.

Gotta find some money, somehow, he mused. Cain't wait till spring, even if I could run the trap line agin. It's kinda peterin' out anyhow. 'Course, I could set up a trap line higher up, I 'spect. That'd take me away two days at a time, though. Have to camp out up there every other night, jist tendin' the thing. Sure hate ta think o' sleepin' alone ever' other night. 'Specially in thet kinda cold.

He took a sip of his whiskey, setting it back down. He rotated the shot-glass slowly, studying it. Even if'n I could do thet, it'd take too long, he told himself silently. Three, four months afore I could even start trappin'. Then another four, five months afore I could take the furs in. We'll be plumb outa ever'thin' afore thet.

Egg 'n milk money'll buy food, I 'spect. We kin git by. Problem is, Freda thinks we got a lot o' money somewheres. Dunno what ever made 'er figger thet. If'n I tell 'er we're busted, an' Steinhaus ain't gonna give us no more credit, she'll be fit to be tied. She'll ream me good. Jist as well figger on sleepin' in the barn fer a month!

He sipped his whiskey again. He shook his head, deliberately diverting his attention from his problems. He eyed the four men at the table next to him, straining to hear what they were saying.

'I ain't kiddin',' one of the men said to his obviously sceptical companions. He wore common work-trousers, but an old, worn, army shirt. 'That's the way it's sent every time.'

'That don't make no sense,' a man in worn cowboy attire responded. 'I mean, without even no guard.'

'Maybe that's so nobody thinks it's anything special,' a third cowboy offered.

'Best way to hide somethin' is right out in the open,' the fourth man suggested.

'But that much money?'

'Seems like an awful chance, to me.'

'Never been a problem yet.'

'How come they send it on the La Bonte stage?'

The ex-soldier shrugged his shoulders. 'No idea. Maybe that's part o' the genius o' the thing. Nobody'd expect a whole fort's payroll to be on a regular stage. Nobody'd expect it to be sent without a detachment o' soldiers for guards. Nobody'd expect it to be on the La Bonte stage. So nobody pays any attention. Then from Casper it goes out to Fort Fetterman under military guard, and nobody even wonders how it got to Casper in the first place.'

'All in gold?' one of the cowboys asked.

The ex-soldier shook his head. 'Nope. Some gold. Mostly paper money. Ain't as heavy. All in one strongbox. Cap'n Gallagher, he tol' me they just toss the strongbox up on top, like it ain't nothin', an' just leave it there till they get here. He said he didn't think the driver even knew how much money was in it.'

'Still don't make no sense to me,' one of the cowboys objected.

'Does to me,' his companion argued. 'Don't make no fuss, and nobody thinks it's anythin' to worry about.'

'Ain't too many stages get held up anyhow. Nobody wants to mess with a shotgun.'

'You ever been on that La Bonte stage?'

'No way! Why in thunder would I ride on a stage coach?'

'Most godawful way to travel anyone ever dreamed up,' another agreed.

'I rode that stage once,' the other responded.

'You did? How come?'

'Got hung up in town. Drank up all my money. Hocked my saddle. Got a letter offerin' me a job up here. Sold my horse to get my saddle outa hock, then had to ride the stage all the way up here to go to work.'

'Too much whiskey an' women, huh?'

'You said it. Boy, lemme tell ya, though, there's a whore there in the Green Bottle saloon that'll make you forget all them long lonely nights in a bedroll.'

'Till you run outa money.'

'Till I run outa money,' he agreed. 'Anyway, that's quite a stage ride. I wasn't sure the team could pull that thing all the way up the pass.'

'Steep road all right.'

'Steep ain't no word for it! When they get to the top, there's a spot where they stop, every time. Right on top. Let the team blow a while, afore they start down the other side. Like some sorta routine. They stop the stage. Driver says, real loud, "We'll be stoppin' here a bit for the horses. Ladies kin go over in the timber to the left, if you need to relieve yourselves. Men kin go over in the trees to the right".'

'There was women on the stage?'

'They wasn't nobody but me! Driver says he always announces it that way though. He told me I was the first passenger they'd had for two weeks. They pert-neart never have more'n one. Quite a bit o' freight, though. I guess that's what they make their money on.'

'So everyone just walks away from the stage, with all that money on it?'

'Yep. 'Course, the driver an' guard don't go that far. Not so far they can't see the stage, I mean. There's a spot with some brush there, where they can just see the stage if they stand up tall. Soon's they relieve theirselves, they come right back.'

'That's gotta be a lot o' money to just leave it settin' there.'

'Like I say, it's always there. Gotta be pertneart ten

thousand dollars, three days afore the first of every month.'

'You know what we oughta do?'

'What?'

'We oughta drift over there an' rob the thing!'

'Yeah, right! An' meet the business end o' Curly's shotgun? Not me.'

'I ain't afraid o' the shotgun,' another protested. 'If'n I was a mind to rob somethin', I'd just shoot him first. There's only two of 'em.'

'It'd be easy enough to do,' the other agreed. 'If you didn't mind bein' on the run the rest o' your life. Besides, who could just up an' shoot somebody?'

'That's the burr all right. I ain't never been on the wrong side o' the law. Ain't about to start now.'

'Me neither. My ma'd turn over in her grave if she thought I'd do somethin' like that.'

'I dunno,' the ex-soldier argued. 'I think, with that much money, every time my conscience squealed, I could just bury it in money till I couldn't hear it.'

'Or stay drunk enough not to worry about it.'

Lang quickly tossed off what was left in his shot-glass. He rose and sauntered out the door, trying to appear as casual as possible. Thoughts were tumbling over each other in a jumbled rush. Three days afore the end o' the month. Thet's three days from now. It's a good day's ride, over there. I know jist where thet thar spot is, atop thet pass. Ten thousand dollars! Thet's all the money we owe an' a whole herd o' cows besides.

He climbed up on to the seat of the wagon and yelled to his team. They left town at a trot, and he scarcely let them slow until he reached home.

It was already dark when he drove into his yard. He hurriedly took care of the team, then began carrying things into the house. Freda came out to help him.

'Did you get everything?'

' 'Course I did. Why?'

'Oh, I don't know. I just thought you acted worried. I didn't know if we had enough money to get all the things I wanted.'

'I tol' you not to worry your purty head 'bout money,' he chided. 'Ain't nothin' too much fer my woman.'

She giggled appreciatively and kissed him lightly. Promise o' things to come, he exulted to himself.

She did not disappoint him. He waited until morning to tell her his plans.

Over the breakfast-table he said casually, 'I 'spect I'd oughta meander up to the other place fer a day er two.'

'Why?'

'They's some fixin' needs done on the corral an' on the roof o' the house.'

'Why do we need to keep it fixed up so well?'

'Cain't let it jist fall apart. When we git squared around so's we kin buy a herd o' cows, we'll need thet house fer a bunkhouse, er fer a married hand.'

'Where are we going to get money enough to buy a whole herd of cows?'

He grinned at her. 'That's what else I found out in town yesterday.'

'What?'

'Got a letter from a lawyer in South Carolina.'

'A letter?'

'Yup. 'Member me tellin' ya 'bout my Uncle Roscoe?'

'No. I don't remember you ever mentioning him.'

'Really? I'm sure I did. He's the one with the store an' all, an' no kids. Anyway, he went an' died, an' heired me some money.'

Her eyes brightened immediately. 'Really? How much?'

'He didn't say. I'm expectin' several thousan' though.'

'Several thousand? Oh, honey. Several thousand dollars. Oh, sweetheart, we can afford to turn my homestead into a real ranch! With hired hands and everything!'

'Well, let's don't go gettin' in too big a hurry!' he protested. 'I ain't rightly sure how much is there, till it's in the bank.'

'It'll come to the bank?'

'Yup. It'll come to the bank in Casper. Anyhow, I still got to get the work done up on the other place. I'll take two er three o' the saddle horses, too.'

'Why do you need them?'

'Oh, jist to ride 'em a bit. Git 'em some fresh grass. They need used, er they'll git fat 'n lazy.'

'Oh. Well, don't stay gone too long. I can't show my man how much I appreciate the life he's building for me when I have to sleep alone, you know.'

He remembered the fire in her goodbye kiss all the way to the other place.

At the other place he hobbled one of the horses where he could reach the rich, tall grass along the creek, and the water from the creek. Riding one horse and leading the other, he rode out at a brisk trot.

10

Reaching For Riches

Lang Hart rode swiftly. Every three hours he stopped, allowed his horses to drink from the Platte River, then switched saddle and bridle to the animal he had been leading, to allow the other horse to rest as it was led, unridden.

When he neared the site of the La Bonte stage station, he left the main road. Riding parallel to that road, out of sight, he worked his way alongside its path until he was nearly half-way to the Horseshoe stage station. At that place the road climbed across the highest point in the road from Cheyenne to Casper. In the fading light he studied the road and the pass.

With ease he found the spot where the stage habitually stopped to rest the horses. He paced the area until he found the obvious place used by the driver and guard to relieve themselves. He stood there, looking around.

At last he settled on a site fifty yards away. Moving in a large circle, he approached the spot he sought from the opposite direction. Within a growth of brush, he found a large fallen tree. He squatted behind it. Peering through the branches of the brush, he had a clear view of the spot where driver and guard would be at their most vulnerable. Because the spot he had chosen was nearer the road than they would be, he would be as directly behind them as the screening brush would allow him to be.

Nodding to himself, he moved carefully away. He rode nearly three miles down the mountain until he found a well concealed spot to camp, beside a trickle of water springing from the mountain's rocks. He picketed his horses, cooked some supper over a small, carefully shielded fire, and rolled into his bedroll.

Couldn't be more perfect, he assured himself as he drifted off to sleep. One more day to spare. I'll set up an' check things tomorrow, jist to be sure. Then the next day my cattle ranch walks right inta my hands.

Uncertain what time to expect the stage, he was in his place of concealment two hours after sunrise. He was positive the stage would not leave the Horseshoe station before daylight, and it would not be possible to leave after daylight and arrive before he was set.

He waited in silence for almost three hours before he heard it. The first sound was from the driver, yelling at the six-horse team, urging them on up the long climb. His voice drifted faintly on the breeze at first, but rapidly grew clearer. Within minutes he could hear the creaking of the stage as it tipped and twisted over the rocky road.

Before the stage came into view, he could hear the casual conversation of two men perched on the driver's seat. Then it emerged from the surrounding timber, horses straining to heave it over the last hump of the long upgrade.

The driver didn't even need to tell the horses where and when to stop. Accustomed to the trip, they knew exactly what was expected of them. At the designated spot they simply stopped, blowing and puffing, lowering their heads, eager for the respite.

The driver called out, 'We'll stop here and rest the horses. All you passengers can take advantage of the stop if you want. Ladies can relieve themselves in the timber to the left. Gents can relieve themselves in the timber to the right.'

He set the brake, wrapped the reins around the handle and climbed down. He looked all around, then nodded. 'Clear's ever, Curly,' he said.

Curly, the shotgun guard, nodded. He broke open the breech of the double barrelled shotgun and climbed down. Again without conversation, the two walked away from the stage to relieve themselves.

Walking around the clump of brush that shielded them from the eyes of passengers who weren't there, they stopped. Curly turned and looked back at the stage, his eyes taking in not only it but the area around and behind it as well. Nodding, he laid the shotgun down on top of a large rock. Then, as if on a silent signal, he and the driver turned directly toward the stage, so they could watch it over the top of the screening brush, as they emptied their bladders.

Lang gasped. They turned directly toward him, as they turned toward the stage! They were facing him!

He crouched lower behind the fallen tree. His heart pounded. Blood rushed in his ears. His stomach cramped intolerably. He lay down on his side, curled up and grabbed himself, trying desperately to keep from wetting his pants.

He realized suddenly he was holding his breath. He could hear the two men urinating on the ground. He tried to breathe slowly and silently, while his lungs ached and shuddered for more air.

He raised his head and peered carefully through the screening brush. The two men had finished. Curly was just picking up his shotgun. As they started back toward the stage, they moved to a position no longer directly facing him.

The tension left Lang with a rush. His stomach relaxed. He studied the backs of the two men quietly and calmly. He watched them return to the stage, climb into the seat, and release the brake.

'Everybody back aboard?' the driver called.

He paused a moment as if waiting for an answer from the passengers who weren't there.

'Don't see why you got to do that ever' time,' Curly complained.

'Reg'lation,' the driver responded. The tone of his voice left no room for argument.

Curly snorted anyway. 'Shoulda stayed in the danged army,' he groused. 'That's the way they do things.'

'They's reasons for them reg'lations,' the driver replied. Slapping the reins against the horses' backs, he called, 'Giddup boys!'

With obvious reluctance, the horses leaned into the harness and the stagecoach creaked into motion. In minutes it disappeared on to the downward grade, twisting its way along the road down to the La Bonte station.

Lang stood up. He spat on to the ground. 'Glad I checked it out,' he said aloud. 'Sure thought they'd keep a-facin' away from the stage the whole time.'

Moving swiftly, he walked a circle around the clearing. Almost at once he found another spot just as suitable. A cluster of large rocks afforded a perfect spot for both concealment and resting his rifle. Thin brush between the rocks and the spot where his targets would be, guaranteed whatever part of his body was exposed would still be masked by brush from there. He nodded and returned to his horse, riding back to his campsite.

He waited until an hour later the next day before riding to the pass. When he arrived, he moved into position at once and settled down to wait. He had just consulted his watch and decided it was about time, when he heard the driver's yell, urging the team up the grade.

He lifted the .45 Peabody breech-loading rifle on to the rocks, and tentatively sighted along it. He checked the cartridge in the breech. Then he laid out three more cartridges on the rock just beside him, where he could grab them quickly.

He squirmed around to get situated comfortably,

so he would not need to move until it was time. He removed his hat and laid it on the ground beside him. He could just barely see the very top of the stagecoach above the intervening brush and rocks when it creaked to a stop.

The driver's voice carried easily to Lang's hiding place. 'We'll stop here and rest the horses. All you passengers can take advantage of the stop if you want. Ladies can relieve themselves in the timber to the left. Gents can relieve themselves in the timber to the right.'

Lang could just see his head as he looked around in all directions. 'Clear's ever, Curly,' he said, as Lang silently mouthed the words he knew he was going to say.

Then another voice startled him. 'That was quite a climb.'

Lang could not see the speaker from his vantage point, but he heard the coach creak as the door opened and somebody stepped to the ground. There was a passenger!

'Sure 'nuff is, Mr Prestamer,' the driver agreed. 'Makes a good spot to get rid o' Mrs Wilfred's coffee, though. I'm always just about to bust by the time we make it up the hill.'

As they talked, Lang could hear them coming closer. Then the three men stepped into sight, walking around the clump of brush. The passenger turned his back to the other men and began to relieve himself at once. The driver and Curly went through their routine of checking the stage, setting down the shotgun, then turned back toward the stage and did the same.

The instant they turned their backs, Lang moved. He lifted the rifle without hesitation, set the sights on the center of Curly's back, just between the shoulder blades, and squeezed the trigger.

The .45 Peabody roared like dynamite in the silence of the mountain. The echoes were scarcely returning when Lang had flipped open the breech, ejected the spent cartridge and thumbed in another. He slapped the breech shut and brought the sights to bear on the driver.

At the instant of the shot, the driver had just begun to relieve himself. Curly grunted and pitched forward. In the part of a second it took the driver to realize what had happened, Lang had reloaded.

The driver grabbed for his pistol and started to turn around. He had turned less than half way when the Peabody roared again. The .45 cartridge entered between two ribs, just behind his right arm, and tore its way through his chest cavity, spewing his life on to the ground beside the body of his dead companion.

The passenger had reacted just as quickly as the driver. He whipped aside the coat tails of his broad-cloth suit and drew a Colt single-action revolver. He turned to face where he thought the shots had come from, crouching as he did.

Lang froze as the man turned to face him. Even though he was sure the man couldn't see him through the screening brush, he was facing him! With a drawn gun!

Lang's hand still held the new shell he was starting to thumb into the breech. The breech stood open, waiting to receive it. He couldn't force himself to move. His heart was hammering. He felt a warm, wet sensation crawl down his leg. He fought to keep a sob from breaking through his clenched lips. His knees began to tremble violently.

The well-dressed passenger stayed in his crouch, scouring the brush and timber for movement or sound. He started backing toward the stage, watching, his thumb on the hammer of his revolver. Lang watched, trembling silently.

When the man had moved back almost to the stage, he stood straight. Lang could barely see the top of his head, just enough to know the man still faced him. Then the man turned around.

The instant he turned around, the tension drained from Lang. He stood up, thumbing the shell into the breech as he did. He lifted the rifle to his shoulder. The passenger, with one more quick look around, grabbed the wheel and began to climb up to the driver's seat.

Lang fixed his sights on the man's back, just between the shoulders, and squeezed the trigger. The Peabody roared again. The man grunted, driven against the side of the coach. Then he dropped backward, falling hard on to the ground. Dust swirled up from around him. The horses snorted and stamped, prancing nervously.

Lang ejected the spent cartridge and thumbed in a fresh one. He walked around the cluster of rocks and approached Curly and the driver. He nudged each of them with a toe of his boot, to be sure there was no life in them. Then he walked to the fallen passenger and did the same.

He stood the Peabody on the ground, leaned it against the stage, and climbed up to the top of the coach. The promised strongbox was there, but it didn't even have a lock on it! Frowning, he lifted the hasp and flipped the lid back.

Inside were a collection of letters. Nothing else. He stared into the emptiness of the box. He shook his head. It's empty! he breathed. They ain't nothin' in it! Nothin' atall!

Then he swore. He swore silently, then softly, then screamed obscenities at the empty box. He kicked it from the top of the coach, sending the mail flying all over the road.

He climbed down. He swore again. He looked at the fallen passenger. Well, at least he's got a fine pistol, he muttered. Guess I'd jist as well have that.

He walked to the dead man and unbuckled his gunbelt. He leaned against it to pull it from beneath the man's considerable weight. As it came loose, the man's vest pulled up, exposing a hint of leather.

What's this? Lang muttered.

He leaned over and lifted the man's vest. It's a money-belt! He's wearin' a money-belt! Well, what-d'ya know!

Working furiously, he unfastened the money-belt and hauled it from beneath the man as well. He opened one of the pouches and whistled. Gold! An' them long pouches gotta be paper money! Well, well.

The thought struck him suddenly that he was on a main road. Somebody could come along at any time. He grabbed his rifle, the fallen passenger's gunbelt and money-belt, and bolted for his horse.

Riding swiftly, he returned to his campsite. He retrieved his extra horse, and rode off at a swift trot, paralleling the road. Once past the La Bonte stage station, he moved to the main road where he could ride faster. Riding at a ground-eating lope, he switched horses every two hours.

He was easily half-way home before he found a secluded spot and rested both mounts and himself. After he had made coffee and eaten a swift meal, he extracted the money-belt from his saddle-bag. Some papers bearing the name 'Rutherford Prestamer' he discarded. Then he began counting the money.

When he finished he chuckled. Twelve hundred thirty-seven dollars! he exulted. Now why would a man be carryin' thet kinda money?

Whyever he had been carrying it, it had certainly salvaged an otherwise disastrous effort for Lang Hart.

11
Prosperity's Problems

It was an extra six hours' hard riding to go by way of Casper instead of returning directly home. Lang just didn't know how else to explain the money. If it didn't come through the bank, it could hardly be convincing that it was an inheritance.

By the time he had made that extra ride, deposited the money, then ridden back to his place on Meander Creek, he and his horses were all exhausted. It was nearing sunrise when he turned the two horses out on hobbles along the creek and put the fresh animal he had left behind into the shed.

He staggered into his one-room house and collapsed on the bed. He didn't even bother removing his spurs. The sun was nearing its zenith when he awoke. He washed up, saddled his fresh horse, and headed for home.

Freda met him in the yard. 'I thought you'd be home yesterday. I was about to ride up and see if something was wrong.'

'Naw. Jist more ta do than I figgered. Plumb amazin' how a place kin run down when you're away from it a few weeks.'

'Did you get everything done?'

'Oh, 'nuff, I 'spect. Fer now, anyhow. Sure'm tired, though. Worked my hind end off.'

'Not too tired, I hope.' Her eyes twinkled and danced. 'I've been sleeping alone the last four nights, you know.'

He was even more tired the next day, but somehow he didn't mind. He spent the day working around the yard and tightening up the chicken pen. He found where coyotes or skunks had been trying to dig under the wire, and buried rocks there to thwart their efforts.

Over supper he said, 'How'd you like to take a little trip?'

Freda's head snapped up. 'Trip? Where?'

'Over to Casper.'

'Why would we go to Casper?'

' 'Member, I tole ya 'bout thet inheritance thing?'

'Yeah.'

'Might be the money's come inta Casper, by now.'

'That'd be a day over and a day back. You could do it in a single day without Ralphy and me.'

'Yup. But then you wouldn't git ta see the big city.'

She snorted. 'Big city? Casper? What's it got, three stores and a bank now?'

He chuckled. 'Little more'n that, actually. They

tell me it's growin' fast. Whole row o' stores along the CY trail. Two er three banks. Opry house, too.'

'An opera house?'

'That's what I hear. Folks come through, time ta time, put on them melerdramas there.'

'Really? Oh, I'd love to see one of those. Could we really go?'

'First thing tomorrow, if'n we kin git someone to look after the chickens an' milk the cows.'

'I'm sure Tilly Maddock would love to do it. Especially if I tell her she can have the eggs and milk while we're gone.'

'I'll ride over'n ask 'er, first thing in the mornin', whilst you're packin' a valise.'

They did the chores in the dark the next morning. By the time the sun peeked over the horizon they were loaded in the wagon, moving out along the road that would lead through the settlement of Fenton's and on to Casper.

Freda's eyes lit up when Lang returned to the wagon. 'We got money,' he announced.

'Oh, Lang! That's such good news. How much?'

'Well, not too much, right now. Seems they's disposin' o' Uncle Roscoe's stuff one thing at a time. There's only 'bout a thousan' here now.'

'A thousand dollars? Really? And more coming?'

'Well, they's s'posed ta be, anyhow, but, yeah, they's a little over a thousan' here now.'

'How much did you take out?'

'Five hunnert.'

'Why so much?'

'Well, we owe Steinhaus two hunnert er so. An' I

gotta get me a new rifle.'

'A new rifle? Why on earth do you need a new rifle?'

'Wal, thet thar ol' Peabody's a purty good rifle, all right enough. It jist takes too long to reload, it bein' a breech loader an' all.'

'Well, why on earth do you need to reload fast anyway?'

He hesitated. 'Wal, 'case I miss a shot, sometimes what I'm aimin' at's gone afore I kin open the breech an' push in another shell. Winchester's got a model 1873 what holds a whole handful o' shells. You jist shoot, jack the lever, an' it's ready to shoot agin, pert-neart as fast as ya kin squeeze the trigger. I aim ta git me one.'

'Well, it certainly seems like a waste of money to me. You already got that new pistol just the other week. And I don't know where you got the money for that, either.'

He interrupted her. 'You wantin' ta shop here in Casper, er head back home an' buy what ya need at Fenton, from Steinhaus?'

'Well, I'm certainly not going to ride this dreadful wagon all the way to Casper and not even shop in the stores that are here!'

By the time they got home, he scarcely had any surplus money after paying off their bill at Steinhaus's general store. He fretted that he had already withdrawn almost half of the proceeds from the stage robbery. But Freda was happy, and when Freda was happy, life was good.

12
The Bragging
Buggy

'Oh, Lang! Look!'

Lang hauled on the reins, bringing the team to a halt. He followed Freda's excited stare.

'What? Where?'

'There! Oh, Lang! It's beautiful!'

'What? The buggy?'

'Of course, the buggy! I've never seen anything so beautiful.'

'Fancy, all right enough.'

'Oh, Lang! I want it!'

'What?'

She elbowed him painfully in the ribs. 'What do you mean, "What?" I just told you what. Lang, I want that buggy.'

'Aw, Freda, thet's ... thet's ... thet thar's a rich fella's buggy.'

'I wonder what kind it is?'

'Studebaker, it says on it.'

'Oh, Oh, Lang' A Studebaker buggy! Do you know, when I was a little girl, there was a banker back home that had a Studebaker buggy. He used to parade through town in that buggy, and his wife sat up there like a queen! And we all stood with our mouths open and stared when they went by. Everybody knew they were the cream of society. They were like ... like royalty, because they had that buggy. Oh, Lang! I'd do anything to have a buggy like that. Anything!'

'Wal, I cain't see how we's ever goin' ta have one. We ain't rich folks, case you forgot.'

'But we could, Lang. You still have that money in the bank in Casper. And there's more coming, you said. And someday we're going to have a cattle ranch, and be the cream of the society here, just like that uppity banker was back home.'

'Wal, thet thar uppity banker owned the bank. We jist got a little money in a bank. They's a whole world o' difference, Freda.'

'Oh, Lang. I thought you loved me.'

'Wal, I do love ya, Freda.'

'But not as much as you love having that money in the bank.'

'It ain't thet atall, Freda. Thet thar money's all we got.'

'I thought you said there would be more coming.'

'Wal, they's s'posed ta be, all right enough, but it ain't thar yet. An' they ain't no tellin' how much thet thar'll end up bein'. Uncle Roscoe, he most likely has lots o' folks ta heir thet thar money o' his'n to.'

'You don't heir money, Lang. An heir is a person.

You will it to an heir. And the heir inherits it, he doesn't heir it. Honestly! You talk as badly as those . . . those homesteaders.'

'We is homesteaders.'

'We are not! We are cattle ranchers on the American frontier.'

'We ain't got no cattle. Wal, 'cept the milk cows.'

'We have beef cattle.'

He snorted. 'Yeah. Twelve head. Some ranch!'

'But we will have more. We will have as fine a herd of cattle as the CY or the Hat Ranch, or any other ranch in Wyoming. And I certainly want to look the part, if I'm going to be the wife of a successful rancher. A cattle baron, that's what.'

'Best work on thet thar first. Then worry 'bout a fancy buggy ta go ta town in.'

'But the buggy is here now. Lang, at least find out who it belongs to. It's obviously for sale. Promise me you'll check into it.'

Lang swiped a hand across his face. 'All right, I'll check inta it.'

'Oh, Lang! I knew I could depend on you. Now let me buy my things so we can go home. While I'm doing that, you can ask around about the buggy.'

He swiped his hand across his face again. 'Wal, I 'spect I'll wait a spell ta do thet thar. I'll ride inta town in a couple o' days an' check it out.'

Freda was less than totally happy with that, but she accepted it. Three days later, tired of answering questions about when he was going to check on that buggy, Lang rode to Casper. He withdrew another five hundred dollars, leaving only a little over a hundred dollars in the account. He rode out at first light, riding swiftly back to Fenton. He entered the general store.

'Well, good morning, Mr Hart,' the storekeeper greeted him.

'Mornin', Mr Steinhaus,' he responded. To himself he muttered, 'Mr Steinhaus. Heavy on the Mr. I don't even know yore name, ya uppity money-bags. I jist git ta call ya Mr Steinhaus, like I ain't on the same level as you atall.'

Aloud he said, 'Thet thar Studebaker yours?'

'Why yes, yes it is. The representative from Studebaker offered to leave it here for a couple months on consignment, actually. I told him I doubted anyone around here would be interested in a conveyance of that extravagance, but he offered anyway.'

'What's it worth?'

'It is quite expensive. Four hundred dollars.'

Lang whistled. 'Four hunnert dollars! Jist fer a buggy.'

'Ah, yes, but it is an investment. When one buys a buggy with the quality of a Studebaker, one can expect not to ever have to buy another within your lifetime.'

'Sure's fancy.'

'It is an extraordinary piece of workmanship. May I guess that Freda has been taken by it?'

'Yeah, she spotted it all right. Thinks she's gotta have it. What's the best price you'd give a fella on it?'

'Are we talking cash, here?'

'Cash on the barrel head.'

'Ah, yes. Your inheritance did come through, I recall.'

'Part of it.'

'I see. Well, perhaps on a cash deal, there would be some room for negotiation. I would be willing to accept three hundred seventy-five dollars.'

'I'll give ya three an' a quarter.'

'Mmmm. My. That wouldn't be possible I'm afraid. The very best I could do would be three hundred sixty-five. And at that, I'm scarcely doing anything other than passing money along with almost no profit to me at all.'

'Three sixty-five, huh?'

'That really is the best I can do.'

'I 'spect as how I could maybe give as much as three forty.'

'Mmmm. No, I really couldn't go that low. Perhaps, since it is a cash offer, I would take three fifty. But that is, absolutely, my final offer.'

'Well, I 'spect I'll take it then.'

'You will? I mean, yes, of course. Did you bring a horse with you to drive it home?'

'Naw. I'll pay ya fer it, an' I'll come in tomorrow er the next day fer it.'

'Very well. You have bought yourself a very, very fine piece of workmanship. Freda will be most proud to be seen in that buggy anywhere. You may have to begin taking her to Casper every month just to show off.'

Lang mumbled something incoherent and paid the storekeeper. Then he mounted up and rode toward Fort Fetterman, instead of going home.

The saloon at Three Mile Hog ranch, near the fort, was bustling with soldiers. Lang ordered whiskey and tossed off the first shot, ordering an immediate refill. He paid for both and made his way to a table toward the back. He had no sooner settled in than a young soldier invited himself to join him.

'Hey, mind if I sit here?'

Lang scowled. 'Free country,' he muttered.

'Thanks,' the soldier replied with a grin. 'Busy place, huh?'

'Always is,' Lang responded. The young soldier gestured toward one of the whores with his beer. 'Ain't they somethin'?'

'Who?'

'The whores in this place. Back East, before I was mustered out to this outfit, everyone talked about the hog ranches and the like out in Wyoming. I honestly expected to see some whores out here that were at least decent to look at. I swear, I haven't seen a woman in this place yet that I'd touch with a ten-foot pole. They've got to be the ugliest, most worn-out bunch of women I ever dreamed of.'

'Wait'll you're out here a couple years,' Lang grinned. 'They'll start ta look plumb good.'

The young soldier laughed and took a drink of his beer. 'That a voice of experience?'

Lang laughed. 'Not my experience. I wouldn't touch one of 'em with a ten-foot pole neither. I ain't that hard up. If'n I was, I'd be plumb scared to death what sorta drip I'd take home ta my wife.'

'You got a wife?'

'Yup. Wife an' son. He's six now.'

'Where do you live?'

'We got a place up Meander Crick.'

'No kiddin! What ya doin' in a place like this, instead of home with your wife?'

'Jist stopped fer a drink. Headin' home shortly. Place is always busy, ain't it?'

'You think it's busy now, you ought to see it right after payday.'

'That so?'

'That is so. We get paid the first of the month. The second of the month this place is jammed out the door, and thirty soldiers standing around the yard. I swear this place has at least half the army's payroll by the end of the second.'

'Thet thar's a lot o' money.'

'That is a powerful lot of money!'

'Wonder somebody don't rob 'em.'

'The soldiers that aren't on active duty are all too drunk. The marshal rides out from Casper the second of every month, like a standing appointment. After Clark closes the place he puts all the money from the month in his saddle-bags and hauls it to Casper, under the protective shotgun of Marshal Jenson Hicks.'

'Thet so? Jist one man a-guardin' all thet money?'

'Two men. Clark ain't no slouch with a gun either, and I don't know anybody that wants to tangle with Hicks. Especially when he's carrying that Greener.'

'How much you 'spect he's haulin'?'

The youngster shrugged. 'Who knows. Just from that one day, it's probably a couple thousand dollars. Add the rest of the month to it, and who knows? Three, four thousand, easy, I'd guess.'

'Lot o' money. Shame ta see all them soldiers wastin' it like thet thar.'

The soldier shrugged again. 'What's the difference? There's whiskey and beer. There's that faro game going over there. And there are the soiled angels of the Hog ranch. Besides that, what is there to spend money on, out here?'

'Not me,' Lang asserted. 'I'm workin' toward buildin' my herd.'

'Good for you,' the soldier responded. 'I'm working on surviving my enlistment so I can go back to Baltimore.'

Lang finished his whiskey and stood. 'Wal, good luck ta ya.'

The soldier silently lifted his beer in return. He was already joined by another soldier before Lang reached the door.

13
Backside Bravery

It claimed the name of Orpah, but it wasn't much. Shacks, tents, and a few more or less permanent buildings had sprung up around Three Mile Hog ranch. So named because it was three miles from Fort Fetterman, it was outside the jurisdiction of the fort command. The nearest law of any kind was at Casper, some thirty miles to the west.

Now it was the center of a hubbub of activity. Soldiers milled around, most of them with a bottle of some kind in hand. Games were being played in nearly every area clear enough to accommodate them. Some played poker on a blanket spread on the ground. Some of those who were still steady enough engaged in contests of speed or strength, with onlookers betting freely on the outcome.

Inside the Hog ranch the saloon's lone room was jampacked. Notably missing from the packed throng were the women. They were being kept as busy as their stamina would allow in the half-dozen small rooms that formed a row next to the saloon. Seldom did a girl finish with a client and make her way back to the saloon before she was engaged by another eager suitor. Most of them simply came to the door of their room when they were ready for the next customer and leaned on the door jamb. Even the most worn of the cadre seldom had time to shift positions before another customer would approach.

Every so often a fight would break out between two of the soldiers. Others would take the precaution of disarming both combatants, then let them fight it out between themselves. There, too, bets were offered and taken on the outcome.

Faced with the boredom of military life on the frontier, lack of places to spend their wages, and the constant possibility of being caught up in a campaign against Indians, it became almost a badge of honor to return to the fort broke, drunk and bloody. This boisterous frenzy became a monthly ritual, the day after payday. It offered the only release from that odd combination of boredom and danger. It afforded one day of distraction, then a common topic of conversation for days to follow as the day's, and the night's, exploits were recounted.

The greatest beneficiaries of the monthly hysteria were the owner of the Hog ranch, the gamblers who gave him a cut to allow their faro games to continue, and the soiled angels, who also gave him a cut to be allowed to ply their ancient trade in this remote pigsty of last resort.

Lang Hart drifted around the fringes of the action. From time to time his lip curled involuntarily at the brazen display of every form of evil.

From time to time a shot would ring out from within the packed interior of the Hog ranch saloon. More often than not, soon after, a body in an army uniform would be carried out, loaded on a horse, and some friend of the deceased would lead the animal in the direction of the fort. The event occurred three times while Lang watched. In none of the three times did the noise level from the interior diminish for more than a couple minutes. It was as if everybody paused to look over the event, then immediately dismissed it and went back to the previous activity.

It was after 3 a.m. when hoofbeats interrupted the festivities. A squadron of soldiers galloped up in the dark. The sergeant in charge fired a gun twice into the air. He called out loudly, 'Time's up! All soldiers fall in. Them as can't walk or ride, find someone to lean on. Back to the fort.'

He remained mounted. The rest of his squad dismounted and swept through the saloon, rousting out every soldier in the place. A couple of them walked along the half dozen doors, banging on them with rifle butts. 'Soldiers all out!' they called at each one.

After they had waited a while, they returned to those still closed and pounded again, then entered. Any errant soldiers still within were herded out, usually clinging to articles of clothing not yet put back on.

Those who had passed out were thrown across saddles and tied in place. A couple of the squad rode around the area, looking for others who might have passed out, or who might have been hiding to wait until the soldiers left.

When all the soldiers had been rounded up, the ragtag collection was herded toward the fort. An eerie silence fell over the place.

Without ceremony the women closed their doors. The gamblers picked up their games, lingered over a last drink, then made their way to their horses and disappeared. A pair of stray cowboys were finally ejected, and the saloon closed down.

In the deep shadows at the end of the building, Lang watched and waited. The noises of cleaning and straightening came through the drafty walls from inside. Then he heard the muffled footfalls of a horse, walking slowly and carefully.

Grateful for the little moonlight available, Lang watched the lone horseman approach. The rider stopped in front of the saloon, and looked around, listening carefully. As he stepped from the saddle, that sliver of moonlight glinted on a marshal's badge on his shirt front.

From the security of the shadows, Lang watched until the marshal was half-way to the door. Then he staggered out from the end of the building. Holding his stomach, he lurched forward, bent double. 'Help me,' he pleaded.

As he asked for help, he pitched forward, on to his face. He struggled back to his knees, staying bent over. 'Help me,' he pleaded again. 'Stabbed me in the gut.'

The marshal released the grip on the butt of his pistol and stepped forward. He bent over. 'Here. Let me see how bad it is,' he said.

As he did, Lang sprang up. A large knife appeared in his right hand. He drove it upward into the marshal's abdomen, reaching for the heart, severing arteries and veins as it reached.

The marshal grunted in surprise and stepped back. He grabbed his stomach, then looked at his hand, surprisingly warm and wet. 'What did. . . ?'

He looked at Lang. A glint of understanding crept into his eyes, but they were already glazing. 'Why. . . ?' he asked, then pitched forward on to his face.

Glancing quickly toward the door, Lang grabbed the marshal by the feet. Grasping both feet, placing himself between them, he dragged the marshal around the corner, into the shadows where he himself had lain in wait.

Moving quickly, he removed the marshal's badge. He pinned it to his own shirt. Then he stepped back around to the front of the building and picked up the reins of the marshal's horse. He walked to the hitch rail and looped the reins over it. He removed the marshal's double-barrelled shotgun from its saddle scabbard and walked to the door.

He tried the door. It was latched from within. He knocked.

'Who's there?' a voice called out.

'Marshal,' he replied.

There was a scuffing of boots, then the grating of wood as the latch bar was removed. The door swung open. Lamplight spilled into the darkness.

The owner of the Hog ranch took a step backward. His hand dropped to his six-gun. 'You ain't the marshal,' he said.

Lang held up his right hand. The double-barrelled shotgun hung loosely in his left. 'Marshal Hicks got hung up. Took a gun-whippin'.'

'Somebody gun-whipped Jenson?'

'Last night. He's OK. Kilt the feller what gun-whipped 'im. He wasn't smart 'nuff to live, nohow. Anyone tries to gun-whip Jenson Hicks ain't smart 'nuff to keep breathin'.'

'I hear you there,' the Hog ranch owner agreed. 'Who're you?'

'Name's Johnson Filmore. Jenson asked me to take 'is horse an' ride on out here ta escort ya back ta Casper. Said you'd be needin' a shotgun escort.'

Clark nodded. 'I was lookin' for him, all right. I sure ain't never heard him mention you, though.'

As they talked, Lang's eyes were taking in the details of the interior. Nobody was there. The place had been reasonably well cleaned up. Fresh sawdust covered the floor.

'Well, I guess it'll be all right,' Clark said. 'I'll holler at my bartender, though, if you don't mind. Just because I don't remember him mentionin' you, I'd feel better if he rides along too.'

'Sure thing,' Lang said.

Clark turned his back and started to walk away, toward the door at the rear of the low-cellinged room. As soon as he turned his back, Lang lifted the double-barrelled shotgun. With no hesitation he

pointed the weapon at the center of the owner's back
and squeezed the trigger.

The gun roared in the close confines of the
saloon. Clark was driven forward on to his knees by
the force of the blast. He stopped momentarily, his
fall arrested by his outstretched hands. Then he
collapsed into the sawdust.

A voice called from beyond the door. 'That you,
Alton? What's goin' on?'

Lang's head jerked up. His eyes darted around the
room. He dived over the bar, landing in the sawdust
behind it just as the door at the rear opened. 'Alton?
What the. . . .'

He heard, rather than saw, the bartender run
across the room and kneel at the side of his boss.
Lang heard him grunt as he rolled the large body of
Clark over. He heard a click as the bartender cocked
the pistol in his hand.

His eyes darting about feverishly, Lang glanced up
at the backbar. He discovered he could see the
bartender in the grimy, cracked mirror. He watched
as the bartender looked around the room carefully,
certain he would be spotted any minute. Once he
thought the bartender looked directly into his reflection in the mirror. He fought down the sob that rose
into his throat.

Unable to look, he buried his face in his hands,
waiting for the inevitable lunge of the bartender to
the end of the bar, where his position would be
exposed and he would be shot. He stayed there,
trembling violently, for what seemed a lifetime.

Nothing happened. Slowly, he lifted his eyes from

his hands. He looked up into the mirror. The bartender was moving, slowly and silently, toward the still open front door.

His back was turned toward Lang! The tension left him with a rush. He calmly stood up, lifted the shotgun to his shoulder, and discharged the contents of the remaining barrel into the back of the burly bartender, some fifteen feet in front of him.

The bartender pitched forward. He grabbed at the door jamb, trying to hold himself up. He tried to turn, lifting his pistol as he did. Lang felt a rising tide of panic resurge within him. Just when he thought it would overwhelm him, the bartender collapsed. He lay on his side, gun extended beyond limp fingers. His eyes slowly closed, as if he were merely drifting off to sleep.

Lang broke open the shotgun. He withdrew the spent cartridges. Beneath the bar he found another, nearly identical shotgun. He extracted the shells from it and reloaded the one he had appropriated from the marshal.

As he replaced the unloaded shotgun, his eyes fell on a canvas bag. He untied the leather thong that held it shut. He opened it. Inside was a collection of bills, gold coins, and an assortment of silver coins. He grinned.

Grabbing the sack, he made his way carefully out the front door. There was no sign of life. He mounted the marshal's horse and rode a half-mile away, to where his own horse waited, tied to a clump of brush.

He dismounted. He knotted the reins on the

marshal's mount together, then looped them over the saddle horn. Then he slapped the animal smartly on the rump. The horse jumped, then trotted off.

Lang mounted his own horse and headed for Casper. Only when he was well away from the Hog ranch did his thighs begin to chafe. He felt his trousers. They were wet.

'Now when did I go an' do thet thar?' he groused. 'Musta been . . . well, no matter. I'll stop an' scrub up good in the first crick I cross.'

14
The Cost of Cattle

'Well, I really think I have a right to know exactly how much money we have.'

'What difference does it make?'

Freda placed her hands on her hips. She leaned forward. 'Well it makes all the difference in the world. I don't know whether we're homesteaders with a Studebaker buggy we can't afford, or whether we're on our way to being cattle barons, like you promised me.'

'We got the buggy 'cuz you wanted it. I didn't. An' anyway, I didn't never promise you nothin' like cattle barons stuff.'

'Well, you most certainly did. You said your Uncle Roscoe had left you a substantial sum of money, although you have never deigned to inform me of any specific amount. It seems to be coming dribbling in to the bank. I never see any papers from the bank. I have no idea what money we have or don't have.'

'I said I'd take care of it.'

'Taking care of it is not what I want from you, Lang Hart. I want to know who I am. I can't possibly know who I am if I don't have any idea how much money I am worth. Now where are you going? You get right back here when I'm talking to you!'

'You want cattle don't ya? I gotta meet up with Henry Renfro. He's got a whole herd he's gotta sell off. Grass ain't good over east, toward Nebrasky. He's lookin' to sell off his whole herd, so's he kin buy agin when the grass comes back.'

'A whole herd. How many? How much money will a whole herd cost? Do we have that much money? Are we going to have hired hands? Lang, I need to know these things. Lang! Get back here and. . . .'

He let the door slam, cutting off the torrent of her words. He slouched to the barn, saddled his horse, and rode out of the yard at a brisk trot.

Two days later he sat on a knoll overlooking a herd of nearly a thousand cows. At his side sat Henry Renfro.

'Fine lookin' cows, Mr Renfro.'

'They're a fine herd,' Renfro agreed. 'I've bred 'em careful. Hate like sin to have to get rid of 'em, but it don't make sense to try to haul hay in from somewhere just to keep 'em alive. Makes more sense to sell off, then buy back when the grass comes. I got about six, seven hundred head I'm keepin'. I got grass enough along the cricks for that many, easy enough.'

'Thousan' head there?'

Renfro nodded. 'Give or take a few head. At least nine fifty. No more than ten fifty.'

'Fine lookin' cows,' Lang repeated.

'Love to sell 'em to you,' Renfro stated.

'All bred?'

'Yup. Oh, they's a few open, I'm sure. I got good bulls, though. Don't end up with many open. Have a few late calves, o' course. Ones that don't take first time around. Not many after that, though. I had pertneart eighty per cent calf crop last year, in spite o' coyotes an' everything.'

'That's good.'

'That's dang good.'

'How much?'

'Four dollars a head.'

'Four thousand fer the herd?'

'Four thousand for the whole herd, give or take a little, depending on the final count, of course.'

'Bulls too?'

'Well, no. I don't want to get rid o' my bulls. Anyway, this is the second year the same bulls has bred this herd. You'll be wantin' different bulls next year anyway. They'll be breedin' back some o' their own heifers, if you don't.'

'Uh huh. Wal, I'll think on it.'

'Don't think too long. I got to be doin' somethin' with 'em pretty quick.'

'Uh huh. I'll be lettin' you know in a few days.'

'Fair enough. I'll hold off doing anything for a week or ten days. If I don't hear from you by then, I'll have to drive 'em to the railroad and ship 'em East for slaughter, I expect.'

As he rode away, Hart did mental arithmetic and growled. Four thousand dollars! Even after thet thar

Hog ranch, I ain't got but thirteen hunnert in the bank. I gotta do somethin', though. Freda, she's plumb dead set on havin' a big ranch. Maybe I'll ride up an' look thet thar bank in Kaycee over. I heerd they's always a passel o' money in it.

The next day he dismounted at Doop's mercantile store, directly across the street from the bank in Kaycee. His hands were sweaty. He wiped them on his trousers, and sauntered into the store. He stood inside, watching the bank through the front window.

'May I help you, sir?'

Lang turned and watched the store owner walking toward him. 'Uh, naw. I mean, yeah, but I, uh, jist need ta look around a bit. Pick out some things.'

'Fine. You go right ahead.' With a pronounced limp, the owner returned to the set of shelves on which he was dusting and rearranging merchandise. Lang wandered around the store, mostly watching the bank through the front window.

The town seemed almost deserted. He laid his hand on the counter. The feel of what he had touched drew his attention away from the window. He looked at a plump feather pillow, with striped ticking. He picked it up. Now, thet thar's a fine piller, he muttered. Store-bought piller! I bet Freda ain't never had a piller she didn't make fer herself. I got ta buy this here fer her.

He picked up the pillow and continued to wander around the store. Studying the merchandise on the shelves, he failed to notice he had walked behind the counter. When he turned around, he spotted a large canvas sack sitting on the shelf beneath the counter.

He glanced up at the storekeeper. He was still working on the dusting and sorting, with his back directly to Lang.

Feeling his knees tremble slightly, Lang reached out with his free hand and opened the top of the sack. It was nearly filled with money, neatly bundled and tied!

He jerked his hand away from it. He looked toward the bank. He looked back at the store owner. He was humming softly as he arranged his merchandise. Lang wiped the sweat from his forehead, unaware he was using the feather pillow to do so.

Abruptly he nodded his head. His hand swept the Colt single action .45, that he had taken from the dead body of Rutherford Prestamer, the passenger on the stagecoach. Without realizing it, his left hand moved over to shield the gun. The pillow moved over and in front of the gun barrel.

Watching the store owner, Lang squeezed the trigger. The gun fired with a muffled thump, scarcely louder than a heavy step of a boot. The store-owner gasped and fell forward. He grabbed the shelves to catch himself from falling. He fell anyway, pulling the shelves down on top of him.

Frowning, Lang looked at the pillow. Feathers were strewn across the store. Can you beat thet thar? he marvelled. Didn't hardly make no sound atall, with thet thar piller over it. Whatdyaknow!

He holstered his gun, dropped the pillow, grabbed the canvas bag, and started for the door. Just then a black, velvet-covered case, that had rested beside the money-bag, caught his eye. He stopped and picked it up. He opened it. Inside was a Confederate Silver Cross. The store-owner was a Confederate war hero! So thet thar's where he got thet limp, Lang mused.

He closed the case again and dropped it in his pocket. Picking up the bag of money, he walked out the front door, mounted his horse, and rode away.

Half a day out of town, he counted the money. It amounted to more than $5,000. He sat on a large rock, mulling his options. Finally he put the money in his saddle-bags and buried the canvas bag under a large rock. He rode back to Renfro's place and paid for the herd of cows, arranging for them to be driven to his place by Renfro's hands in two weeks.

15

Realism Rides the Rancher

'Who's going to feed them?'

Lang faced his wife. She glared back at him, hands on her hips. 'Wal, I 'spect that'd be you,' he stated.

'How can I cook for cowboys and still take care of all the chores? What do you think I do around here all day? Do you know how much work it is to keep all the chores done, take care of the milk cows and the chickens and pigs, and keep the laundry done, and watch Ralphy, and everything else? How on earth do you think I'm going to find time to cook for a crew of hungry cowboys?'

'Wal, what else we gonna do?'

'Build a bunkhouse, with a cookhouse on one end, and hire a cook, of course. Like any big ranch does.'

'Wal . . .' he hesitated.

'Wal, nothing,' she retorted. 'That's just what we have to do.'

'But that thar's a passel o' money! We gotta have three er four hands, ta handle thet many cows. Then we gotta have a hayin' crew put up hay, er we ain't gonna have nothin' ta feed 'em, come winter. Thet thar means half a dozen others, till frost or so. Then if we add a cook, that means we'll be hirin' pertneart a dozen guys. Even at thirty bucks a month, thet thar's, uh, let me see . . .'

'Three hundred sixty dollars a month in wages,' she supplied for him. 'For five months, would add up to eighteen hundred dollars. Then you'll need five hands the rest of the time, which is one hundred fifty dollars a month. That will be for about a full year, until time to sell the calves, which will be another eighteen hundred dollars. That's thirty-six hundred dollars. Then you'll need the money for the haying crew for next summer, too, before it's time to sell calves. That will be another thousand. And it will probably cost almost a thousand dollars to have the bunkhouse and cookhouse built. When you add in the other expenses and what it costs us to live as well, we will need about six thousand dollars to tide us over until we sell calves the first time. We do have that much money, don't we?'

Mentally Lang measured her rapid-fire addition of their needs against the less than $3,000 they had in the bank. Only half enough. Why was it never enough? No matter what he did, no matter how many lucky breaks he hit, there was never money enough. Worse than that, every time he launched out with another plan to steal more money, he came back feeling lower than a snake's belly. In a word, he hated himself. He hated what he was doing. He hated his cowardice. Why couldn't they have just stayed small-time homesteaders? He was so happy with the achievement of building the two houses. A homestead was something he could be proud of. Why did Freda have to be so set on being the wife of a cattle baron?

Even as the question posed itself in his mind, he remembered the aching loneliness of life without her. He remembered, after he had found her, returning to the emptiness of his own home, and how the loneliness had consumed him. He felt a pang of loneliness for his dead friend, and felt again the rush of relief that he was, at least, innocent of that death.

He remembered as well the contrast of life with Freda when she was happy and when she was not. When she was happy with her lot and with what he supplied her, life was a honeymoon of joy and contentment. When she was unhappy because she was denied something she wanted, life was worse than the loneliness of his former existence.

'Uh, it'll cut us purty close, I 'spect,' he said. 'But we oughta make it all right enough.'

'For the tenth time, I just wish you would turn over the handling of the finances to me,' she insisted. 'I have a much better head for figures, and I could obviously do a better job of it than you can.'

He bristled. 'An' fer the tenth time, thet thar ain't gonna happen,' he insisted just as vehemently. 'I'm the man o' this here house, an' handlin' the money's part o' bein' the man o' the house. Did you figger anythin' fer hayin' 'quipment?'

Her eyes lost the bright thrust of anger and became reflective. 'Oh, no. I didn't even think of that. We'll have to have a couple mowers, rakes, a haystacker, and probably, what, another six or eight workhorses?'

'An' a horse barn, to take care o' as many horses as we're gonna need,' he added.

'Oh, dear! Then we're going to be closer to ten thousand dollars that we need, aren't we?'

'Thet thar's what I figger,' he said. 'Thet thar's what I been tryin' to stay under, anyhow.'

Her voice reflected a level of wonder. 'We have ten thousand dollars?' she asked.

'Uh, wal, like I said, all thet thar stuff's gonna run us plumb close. I 'spect it'd make sense fer me ta go ta Cheyenne to get all thet thar hayin' 'quipment, an' such. We kin hire Virgil Olson fer the buildin' o' the bunkhouse an' barn. They say he's got a sawmill he kin haul in an' set up, an' he kin make cut lumber outa logs right here on the place to build 'em with.'

'A sawmill? Right here?'

'Wal, not right in the yard, mind ya, but right here on the place. Thetaway, he kin build ever'thin' outa cut lumber, steada logs.'

'Oh, that would be wonderful. Then we could have buildings that reflect the prosperity of a real ranch! Oh, Lang! You really are wonderful. You make me feel like a queen. You don't have to go to Cheyenne today do you? Could you wait until tomorrow? I really don't want to sleep alone tonight.'

Later, while Freda slept contentedly beside him, Lang stared into the darkness. How was he going to come up with $10,000? The bank at Kaycee beckoned, but he dismissed the idea. So soon after his robbery and murder of the storekeeper right across the street from the bank, a stranger in town would be watched closely. More than anything in the world he feared being watched.

He finally reached a decision to go to Cheyenne as he had suggested. In addition to buying the haying equipment he needed, probably at a much better price than he could get from Steinhaus, he could watch for opportunities there. Such opportunities were always present, he had found, for anyone willing to act swiftly, decisively, and without hesitation. And those who were shot from behind were not only unable to tell who had shot them, they didn't even know.

When he finally fell into a fitful sleep, his slumber was punctuated by dreams. In every dream, just as he prepared to shoot someone, that person would turn and look at him. Then his fear would return. He would stand, petrified, unable to respond as the person laughed at him, laughed at the evidence of his fear that stained his pants' legs. Then the person always drew a gun, and shot him. With the firing of the gun in each dream, he woke with a start, bathed in cold sweat. With effort he returned to sleep, only to wake, terrified, from a similar dream.

At breakfast, Freda was solicitous. 'What's wrong, darling? I thought you'd sleep like a log, after last night. You look like you didn't sleep a wink.'

'Aw, jist thinkin' 'bout too many things,' he groused. 'Worryin' 'bout findin' good hands, gettin' the 'quipment freighted up here, that kinda thing.'

She came up behind him where he sat at the table. She wrapped her arms around him. She nuzzled the side of his neck. 'You'll work it all out,' she assured him. 'I am so lucky to have such a strong, brave husband to keep me happy and provide so well for me. Don't stay in Cheyenne any longer than you need to. I'll be waiting for you to get home.'

Tired as he was, he felt desire stir within him. He dismissed the dream, and began planning his trip to Cheyenne.

16
Bank Withdrawal

Cheyenne was a bustling town. The constant furore of activity seemed frenetic to Lang. It made him tired, just watching so many people hurrying all the time. Although he had been born and raised in a larger city than Cheyenne, he remembered life there as being slower, easier, more relaxed.

He found two separate dealers for haying equipment. Over the space of four days, going back and forth from one to the other, he had dickered effectively. The asking price for the machinery had been reduced by easily a third. When he finally settled on the McCormick mowers, rakes and stacker, they had been loaded on to the large wagon he had driven all the way to Cheyenne for the purpose. He had paid for everything with cash, and was keenly aware it was almost the end of his money.

As he had dickered for the equipment, he had carefully watched the two banks Cheyenne boasted. He noticed in particular that the First Mercantile

Bank of Cheyenne opened for business at 7 a.m. In the time he had been there, he had not noticed a single customer approach the bank before 9 a.m., the time the other bank opened. That meant they were open for fully two hours before their first customer arrived.

By 6 a.m. the next morning he was ready. The team was hitched to the wagon, piled high with dismantled haying equipment, tied firmly in place. Lang took a feather pillow he had purchased from a small store on the way to Cheyenne. He carefully cut the stitching at one end. Removing half the feathers, he let the incessant Cheyenne wind blow them away from behind the hotel. Then he replaced them with a brick he had picked up the day before. Twisting the pillow-case shut, he hefted it. It looked and felt like a pillow-case stuffed with currency, and perhaps some gold. He nodded with satisfaction.

At five minutes past seven, he tied up the team in front of the bank. He walked in, carrying the pillow-case. The teller looked up, faintly surprised to have a customer so early. Through the bars of his cage he said, 'Good morning. May I help you?'

'Uh, well, yeah,' Lang replied. 'I, uh, was thinkin' some o' puttin' my money in the bank, 'stead o' keepin' it at home.'

'A wise decision,' the teller enthused. 'Set it up here, and we will count it all out, place it on deposit, and issue you a receipt.'

'Uh, well, I was wonderin' . . . Are ya sure it's safe here?'

'Oh, my, yes. It's as safe as modern technology can

make it. Kept in that vault, of course, and locked securely at night.'

'What 'bout robberies?'

'Oh, we have never had a bank robbery in Cheyenne! No, your money is perfectly safe here. Now if you will just hand it up here . . .'

'Uh, wal, I ain't sure. I 'spect I'd like ta talk ta the president o' the bank a bit, afore I go puttin' all this in here.'

Irritation showed plainly on the teller's face. 'Well, that really isn't necessary at all. I am the chief teller, and perfectly capable of handling a simple deposit.'

'Wal, no offence er nothin', but I'd be easier in my mind an' all if I could talk with him a few minutes.'

The teller compressed his lips tightly. 'Oh, very well. I will see if Mr Goldsworthy has time to talk with you. One moment please.'

He whirled on his heel and stalked to a door three or four steps behind the teller's window. He tapped softly. At the sound of a muffled response, he opened the door. He stepped in and swung the door almost shut. Nonetheless, Lang could hear him clearly.

'There is a man out here with a pillow-case full of money that he has obviously kept hidden in his home. He wishes to deposit it, but insists upon speaking with you first.'

'Very well,' the bank president responded. 'Send him in.'

Without answering, the teller emerged from the small office. He held the door opened, beckoning Lang around the end of the counter and toward the door, 'You may come around and come in, sir,' he said. His voice was both haughty and offended. 'Mr Goldsworthy will see you now.'

Lang rounded the end of the tall counter and entered the office. He clutched the pillow-case tightly. The president of the bank met him with an expansive, 'Come right on in, sir. Come right in. Here, have a chair. I am honored you have come to us as the institution to care for ... am I right in assuming this is a life's savings?'

'Uh, yeah. Yes sir. Spent my whole life savin' up. Ain't never trusted banks afore. Jist gettin' kinda skittish 'bout keepin' this much money hid on the place, ya know.'

'Oh, I understand that perfectly well,' Reginald Goldsworthy assured him. 'Perfectly well. But I can assure you, this bank is totally trustworthy. We have nearly a million dollars on deposit here. Nearly a million dollars! We invest it shrewdly and wisely. We pay a full per cent interest on deposits as well. Your money grows while it's kept safe and sound.'

As the bank president escorted him to a chair, he swung the door shut and latched it. Lang looked around at the small office. In a place of utmost prominence was a document that bore the name of Harvard University. Lang nodded toward it. 'You git a eddication at thet place?'

Mr Goldsworthy beamed. He rose from his chair. 'Yes, Indeed I did. Harvard University. Finest in the land, if I do say so.'

As he spoke, he walked to the diploma. He lifted it from its nail and held it with both hands, studying it. His back was directly toward Lang.

Lang acted swiftly. With no hesitation, as though he had carried out the action a hundred times in his mind, he rose silently from the chair. He drew his pistol. He thrust the pillow against the front of the gun-barrel, pointed at the bank president's back. He thumbed back the hammer of the pistol and tried to squeeze the trigger. Suddenly a series of pictures flashed in his mind. In an instant he saw Spud Whitaker fly from the corral fence into the path of the angry bull. He saw the old sergeant turn and look at him quizzically, then his eyes glazed over and he fell to the ground. He saw Prestamer driven forward into the side of the stagecoach, then slump to the ground. He saw the Kaycee storekeeper limping across the floor of his store for the last time. Sweat erupted on his face.

He lowered the hammer on the pistol and stepped forward. He swung the pistol, striking the bank president hard across the side of his head. Goldsworthy dropped the diploma and fell forward against the wall.

Lang listened carefully. No sounds of alarm issued from the bank beyond the door. He stepped to the door. He slowly and silently lifted the latch. He opened the door an inch and peered through the crack. The teller stood at his cage, back toward the door, busily adding up figures on a sheet of paper.

Lang swung the door open. He dropped the pillow on the floor. He took three swift steps forward. He brought his gun barrel down hard on to the teller's head.

The teller gasped and fell forward across the counter. He slid downward, collapsing in a heap.

Lang holstered his pistol. He grabbed up the pillow and dumped the feathers from it. He walked quickly to the vault. Looking around, he began quickly opening drawers. All the currency he found he transferred swiftly into the pillow case. It took less than five minutes for him to gather as much currency as he could readily carry in the bag.

He walked to the front door. Noticing a sign hanging in the glass of the front door, he swung it so he could read 'open' lettered on it. He turned it around, so it would read 'closed' from outside. He stepped out. He shut the door carefully behind him.

He walked casually to his heavily laden wagon. He stuffed the pillow-case filled with money into a hollow spot near the front of the wagon. He climbed into the seat, picked up the reins, released the brake, and clucked to the team. They leaned into the harness and the wagon began the long trip back to Meander Creek.

At Orpah, Lang retrieved a saddle horse he had left there. He turned the team over to the livery barn, telling the proprietor he would return for them in two days. Saddle-bags bulging with the cash from the discarded pillow-case, he mounted the horse for the trip to Casper. He would be able to deposit more than $8,000. Then he would return to Freda, and work on the horse barn, the bunkhouse and the cookhouse could begin. With a start he realized his herd of cows would arrive in less than three days.

17

The Law's Arm Reaches

Dust hung in the quiet air. The soft footfalls of horse and dog raised tiny clouds of the white dust, but they settled back to earth quickly and silently. The rider was well into the yard before the ranch dogs even noticed the strange intruder.

When they noticed, they began barking furiously. A quiet word from the rider shifted his own dog's attention away from them, and he continued obediently at the heels of his master's horse.

The rider's eyes swept the ranch yard, the barn, the bunkhouse, the house. They never seemed to stop probing. When the forty-something rancher stepped to the front porch, those eyes seemed to be already there, waiting for him to appear.

'Mornin', Marshal,' the rancher called out. 'Get down an' come in. You're just in time for breakfast.'

'Mornin', Slim,' the man responded. The morning sun glinted on the marshal's badge on his vest.

'Never turned down a meal Molly cooked yet. This don't seem a good day to start.'

The rancher grinned. 'I gotta warn you, though, Marshal. Eat too many o' Molly's meals and you'll start to sport a gut like I got.'

He patted his slightly bulging stomach appreciatively as he said it. The marshal dismounted, dropping the reins of his horse carelessly across the hitch rail. He spoke softly to his dog. 'Stay here, Fred.'

The dog immediately dropped to the ground, watching his master, panting contentedly.

Over a second cup of coffee, following a breakfast of fried potatoes, steak and eggs, the marshal said, 'Fine breakfast, Molly. You feed a man like that, he'll just keep coming back, though. You did know that, didn't you?'

Molly Hasacker smiled back at him. 'That's the idea, Y.A. We like your company. Now if I could just persuade you to bring Rebecca along with you when you ride out here, I'd be happy.'

Marshal Y.A. Oliver nodded his head. His great handlebar mustache waggled as he did. 'She'd love it if I could've brought her, Molly,' he agreed. 'We don't get together with you folks very often. Of course, you two could always come to town to visit us, you know.'

Molly snorted. 'Just try to get Slim off the place that long!'

'Aw, Molly,' Slim protested. 'I get you to town often enough.'

'Often enough for whom?' she teased. 'Once a year is often enough to suit you.'

Slim swung his attention back to the marshal. 'What brings you out, Y.A.?'

The marshal sipped his coffee, then brushed at his moustache. 'Just pokin' around,' he said. His voice was careful, thoughtful. 'There's been a rash of killings, and robberies, around lately.'

Molly's eyes mirrored her concern. 'Around here?'

The marshal shook his head. 'No, not really. Just here and there. But there seems to be a pattern, sort of. It seems that folks are getting shot and robbed. That's nothing new, I'm afraid, in this country. But these all bear something of the same pattern. They are all shot in the back. Well, all except a marshal, and he was stabbed. But then two others were shot in the back at the same place.'

'The Hog ranch?'

Oliver nodded. 'Figured you'd heard about it. Marshal from Casper was stabbed. Took his badge. Then Clark was shot in the back with the marshal's shotgun, and so was his bartender. Took all the receipts from the soldiers at Fort Fetterman blowing their month's pay.'

'We heard about it all right. That'd be a pretty good chunk of money, I'd guess.'

'It would at that. Then there was a storekeeper in Kaycee. Shot in the back and robbed, right in his store, in broad daylight.'

'Oh, my!' Molly responded. 'We hadn't heard about that.'

'And a stage was robbed down the other side of the La Bonte station. Same thing. Driver, guard, one

passenger, all shot in the back. Wasn't anything on
the stage, though. Might have been the passenger
that was carryin' money, but his wallet wasn't taken.'

'So why does that bring you out here?'

'Just pokin' around,' the marshal repeated.
'Thought I'd hang around the cookshack and the
bunkhouse tonight, if you don't mind. See if any of
the boys has heard or seen anything. If you spot all
the places these things have happened on a map, it
makes sort of a rough half-circle. This area is right in
the center of that half-circle. Thought it might be
someone from around here, riding off one direction
and another to pull off a robbery, then ducking back
home till things settle down, then doing the same
thing a different direction.'

'Someone on my place, you mean?'

Oliver shook his head. 'Naw, probably not. Might
be someone in the area, though. Have you noticed
anyone in the area having more money than they
ought.'

Slim and Molly looked at each other. Oliver
noticed it immediately. 'I'd take kindly to you telling
me what you've noticed. I wouldn't count it gossip,
and sure wouldn't repeat it.'

Molly and Slim looked at each other again. Molly
nodded her head, almost imperceptibly. Slim cleared
his throat. 'Well, I ain't too comfortable talkin' about
folks.'

'I understand that. On the other hand, somebody
is committing some pretty serious crimes. And, he's a
back-shooter.'

The last words seemed to steel Slim's resolve. He

nodded his head. 'Well, it's just gossip, so I don't want you to think too much of it. But there's a homesteader, six or eight miles up Meander Creek, that seems to be turning from a homesteader into a rancher awfully quick.'

'Really? What's his name?'

'Lang Hart.'

'Been in the country long?'

'Several years. He built himself a fine house on his claim. Small, but a real fine job of building. He's a real worker. Then he helped his neighbor build a bigger one on his claim. Then the neighbor went and got himself killed. Mule kicked him in the head. Danged if Hart didn't marry the widow, pertneart before the other guy was cold.'

The marshal pursed his lips. 'Did anyone see the mule kick him?'

Hasacker shook his head. 'Nope. But it was the mule, all right. The print of the mule's hoof was plain as day in his head. Them mules has got a powerful kick. Put a hole plumb through his skull. Killed him instantly.'

The marshal nodded. 'Then they seemed to come up with a lot of money?'

Hasacker nodded again. 'They were struggling along, like everybody else, for quite a while. Had a few milk cows and sold the milk, raised chickens and sold the eggs, even had a couple old sows and a boar. Raised a few oats along the crick. But they was gettin' further and further behind. Steinhaus was just about to cut off their credit, when they come up with a bunch of money. Said some inheritance come through. An uncle of his in South Carolina or North Carolina. Never can keep them two straight. Anyway, they paid off their bill, started buyin' stuff, and been pretty prosperous every since. Even bought themselves a fine Studebaker buggy.'

'No kidding?'

'I can't afford a Studebaker,' Slim asserted.

'About when did this inheritance come through?'

'Must've been pertneart two years ago.'

'Just about the time the stage was robbed,' the marshal mused.

'You think he mighta done that?' Slim asked.

'I have no idea,' Oliver responded. 'Just tryin' to fit things together. Were there other times he came up with sudden money?'

'Now that's hard to say,' Hasacker hesitated. 'He did kind of spend money in spurts. Biggest one was when he bought that whole herd of cows, then hired almost a dozen hands, including the carpenters.'

'Carpenters?'

'Yeah. Buildin' a big horse-barn. Bunkhouse. Cookhouse too, I hear. Bigger'n mine, from what they say.'

'Lot of buildin' for one time.'

'Got to, I 'spect. He bought a herd of cows long before he was set up to take care of 'em. Then he had to have hands to look after 'em, wean the calves, put up hay, all that. He didn't have any place for any of them to live, except his own house. That's about four miles from his wife's homestead, and it's just a one-room house. So he has to have the barn and the bunkhouse and everything, all right now.'

'But that takes an awfully lot of money. If he got an inheritance a couple years ago, why is he just now doing all that, I wonder.'

'Claims he didn't have it all then. Something about the estate being sold off a piece at a time.'

'That seems strange.'

'Different than I ever knew an estate to be done, but down South, after the war, who knows how they might be doing things.'

'True enough. Well, if you don't mind, I'll sort of keep my ear to the ground when your boys all come in for the evening. Still got that black woman cookin'?'

'Sure do. She'll never leave here. Likes being treated like a regular woman. Gonna have to build another house on the place, though, if I read the signs right.'

'That right? Why's that?'

'Well, you know that black cowboy I got?'

'Walker?'

'Isaiah Walker,' Slim confirmed. 'He just went plumb googly-eyed over Beulah when we brung her out here. Can't hardly get him out of the cookhouse to do any work. Gonna have to make 'em get married, just so I can get any work out of the man.'

'You could do worse,' Oliver affirmed. 'That'd give you a right stable cook and hand both.'

'You might talk to him,' the rancher suggested.

The marshal's eyebrows lifted. 'Why's that?'

'Well, I heard, roundabout, that he might know that Lang fellow.'

'I'll check it out,' Oliver promised.

18

Invisible Eyes, Silent Ears

'Well, hello, Isaiah,' the marshal greeted.

The black cowboy jumped from his chair. He had been sitting backward on the chair, leaning on the chair's back, talking with the cook.

'Oh, well, good mawnin', Mistah Marshal,' he stammered. 'I was just on my way out. Mistah Hasacker, he wants me to check on them yearlin's over in the south meadow, and I was just on my way.'

Beulah Jones laughed at his obvious embarrassment. 'Oh, what you be tryin' to tell the marshal, Isaiah? I bet he already know Mistah Hasacker can't get you outa my cookhouse to do no work, without sendin' someone to drag you out. You keep hangin' 'round here till I swear you gonna get yourself fired and me too. Then I ain't gonna have no job, and what am I gonna do then?'

'Fact is, I was hopin' to catch you here,' the marshal interrupted.

Isaiah's eyes suddenly grew wider. 'You was?'

'Got time for a cup of coffee?'

'Mistah Marshal,' Beulah interrupted, 'he already done drunk so much coffee he'd float outa here if his feet wasn't so heavy.'

Oliver grinned. 'Well, then, I guess another cup couldn't hurt.'

Isaiah's eyes darted back and forth between the marshal and Beulah. He sat down uneasily across the table from the marshal. Beulah carried two steaming cups of coffee, sitting one in front of each man. 'Thank you, Beulah,' the marshal responded.

'You be plumb welcome, Marshal Oliver,' she answered. 'Now don't you go bein' too hard on my man, Isaiah. He ain't in no kinda trouble is he, Mistah Oliver?'

'No, he's in no trouble,' the marshal assured her. 'Don't worry about him.'

'Then why you wantin' to talk to me?' Isaiah queried.

'You're an observant man,' the marshal said. 'I was hoping you could help me out with some information.'

Isaiah's wariness increased visibly. 'What kinda information, Marshal?'

Y.A. Oliver sipped his coffee thoughtfully. He did not answer the question. 'A black man is in a unique position,' he observed. 'Especially, I have noticed, with people from the South. They tend to ignore the fact that you exist. If you see anything, or hear something, it doesn't seem to matter. When they look around, they look right through you, as if you weren't there.'

'Yessuh, Mistah Oliver. That's the way it is.'

'That allows you to see and hear things I never would,' the marshal explained. 'And I really need some help. There has been a series of crimes in the area that are particularly heinous.'

'I doesn't know that word,' Isaiah interrupted.

'Heinous means especially bad. Reprehensible. Well, that's probably worse. Just, crimes that are despicable because they are done in a cowardly way.'

'Some people is cowards,' Isaiah agreed.

'How well do you know Lang Hart?' the marshal asked abruptly.

Isaiah jumped as if he had been shot. 'Now why you mention him?'

'I understand he has come into considerable money recently,' the marshal continued. 'Some uncle of his in South Carolina died, and left him a goodly sum. I just wondered what you could tell me about him.'

Isaiah shook his head. 'There ain't nothin' what I can say, Mistah Oliver. I gotta go, though. I gotta get me over to that south meadow and check on them cows.'

'You really need to tell me what you know about Lang Hart first,' the marshal insisted.

Isaiah swallowed hard. He looked toward Beulah, his eyes pleading. She walked over toward the two men. Her hands were covered with flour. She wiped them in her apron as she walked. Her eyes were fixed on Isaiah. 'You best tell him, Isaiah,' she said softly.

'I cain't,' Isaiah replied.

Beulah turned to the marshal. 'Mistah Oliver, you

is a good man. The men all say, when they is talkin' about you, that you is a man of your word. If my man tells you what he knows, will you promise you ain't never gonna tell nobody how you found out?'

'I will give you my word, Isaiah,' Oliver replied.

'They'd hang me, if they knowed I was tellin' tales on white folks,' Isaiah worried.

'I have no reason to ever tell anyone where I learned anything you can tell me. It isn't as if I could ask you to testify in court.'

'Oh, no, Mistah Oliver. I couldn't do that. You know a black man can't say nothin' in court.'

'So if I never tell anyone, and you cannot be forced to testify in court, or couldn't testify in court if you wanted to, you can tell me safely. Who is Lang Hart?'

Isaiah's eyes widened even further. 'You already knows that ain't his real name?'

'I had assumed it. What is his name?'

Isaiah's eyes darted back and forth from Beulah to the marshal. Finally he sighed heavily. He picked up his coffee and took a long drink. He sat it down, wiping his mouth with the back of his hand. He stared silently for a long moment. Then he nodded his head once, as if arriving at a decision.

'His name used to be Lyndon Barnes. He was in the same outfit my massah was in, in the war. The day my massah was kilt, when I got free, he was in that battle at Bull Run. Only he was a coward. He kept on loadin' an' loadin' his gun, an' never ever shootin' it. I don't know what finally happened to it. Next thing I knowed, my massah, he got shot and kilt. So I took the paper what said I was free now, an' I took two guns and a horse, an' I rode outa there.'

'Rode away a free man,' the marshal echoed.

'Free man,' Isaiah repeated. 'Only I hadn't got far when I seen Mistah Barnes talkin' to a sergeant. I think he cut an' run, an' the sergeant was sendin' him back. Anyhow, the sergeant, he turned his back on Mistah Barnes. Then Mistah Barnes pulled his gun out an' shot the sergeant right in the back. Kilt him dead. Then he got on the sergeant's horse an' rode outa there like the devil hisself was after him.'

'Shot him in the back,' the marshal mused.

'Right plumb in the back,' Isaiah agreed. 'Then, a good time later, I was in Mistah Steinhaus's store, away out heah in Wyomin', buyin' me some things. Mistah Barnes, he comes in, like a ghost outa some ol' dream o' mine, and he's arguin' with Mistah Steinhaus about how he needs more credit, an' he's got money comin' from South Carolina. Only Mistah Steinhaus was callin' him Mistah Hart. An' I knowed Mistah Barnes, he was from Virginia, not South Carolina. Then he looks at me, but like you said, Mistah Oliver, they never see a black man when they looks at him. He didn't recognize that I was there at Bull Run with him. All he seen was just a nigger, so he didn't pay no attention.'

'I see. Lyndon Barnes. I will pursue that a little bit. Do you know anything more of him?'

Isaiah swallowed hard. 'Well, Mistah Oliver, I guess I does know one more thing.'

'What's that?'

'Well, Mistah Hopper, the one what got kilt by his mule?'

'Ralph Hopper? Husband to the woman Hart is married to now?'

'Yessuh, Mistah Oliver. Afore Mistah Hopper, he went an' got kicked in the head by his own mule, I seen Mistah Barnes, I mean Mistah Hart, skinnin' in some trees with that team o' mules, for Mistah Hopper.'

'Using Hopper's mules?'

'Yessuh. He worked over there, for Mistah Hopper, a whole lot. I seen him several times, when I was workin' over by there, for Mistah Hasacker, doin' what he sent me to do. An' there was one day when I seen Mistah Barnes restin' his mules. I mean, restin' Mistah Hopper's mules. An' he was tossin' rocks at one of 'em.'

'Rocks?'

'Yessuh. Oh, not big rocks. Jis' little un's. An' ever' time he hit that mule jis' right with a rock, that mule he kicks like ever'thin'. I didn't make no sense how come a man would be makin' a mule kick like that, but he kept on doin' it all the while what I watched.'

Oliver frowned. 'He was throwing a rock, hitting the mule in just the right spot, and every time the rock hit that spot, the mule would kick?'

'Yessuh.'

'So the mule had a hot spot,' the marshal said softly. 'Then all he had to do was get Hopper to bend over at the right spot, throw a rock, and let the mule kill him.'

'Well, that there's sort of what me an' Beulah been thinkin',' Isaiah agreed. 'Only, you know, they ain't nobody I could ever tell that. I jis' sorta slipped off an' away, after I watched hin a while, an' I'm sure he don't never know I see'd him atall.'

'I'm sure he doesn't,' the marshal agreed. 'Well, thank you, Isaiah. You have been most helpful. If you hear or notice anything else, please let me know.'

'Thank you, Mistah Oliver,' Isaiah said. His voice was low, intense. 'I feels so much bettuh, on account of I tol' you 'bout that. It's been sittin' on my heart like a big ol' steer sittin' on me, an' I didn't know so much I could do about it. I feels like a whole load's done been lifted off me.'

He grabbed his hat and bolted for the door.

The marshal followed, slowly and thoughtfully. 'Thanks for the coffee, Beulah,' he called over his shoulder.

19

Big Plans Cost Big Money

'Oh, Lang! Isn't it going to be magnificent?'

Lang Hart looked like he had a sour stomach. 'They ain't no need to have it thet big.'

'Oh, but we will need it that big,' Freda insisted. 'And have you ever seen a finer horse barn? There are thirty stalls! Thirty, sweetheart! And two big rooms for saddles and everything. And six stanchions for milk cows. And that's especially nice, since we have a hired hand to milk them, and I don't have to any more. And room in the hay mow for enough hay for all winter. And oats, too. Did you see the oats chute?'

'I seen it. Anyhow, you tol' me all 'bout it when Virgil first tol' ya how he could do it.'

She continued as if he didn't know anything about it. 'Isn't that just the most wonderful thing? Put your bucket under the chute and pull the rope, and oats just pour down. Pull the other rope and it shuts them off. And the grain bin in the hay mow will hold over five hundred bushels of oats. Five hundred bushels!'

'Ain't never hurt me to scoop up oats out'n a bin to dump in the trough fer the horses.'

'But anyone can do that,' she dismissed.

'But somebody's still gotta scoop all them oats clear up there.'

'Oh, that's another thing! See that big hopper? It has that rig and ring that fastens to the rope on the hay mow hoist. Just like the hay hoist. It's filled with oats, then the team pulls the rope to hoist it up, then you can pull it in on the track and just dump it in the grain bin. It doesn't even have to be shovelled up there.'

'I hadn't noticed thet thar. Purty fancy, all right. Purty 'spensive, too.'

'Oh, but I knew I could have Virgil add those things, and make the barn bigger than we had planned. I knew you wouldn't mind. You were gone for a couple weeks, and the foundation was all done before you got back. That's when he had to know how big to make it. And we do have the money, don't we? You never have told me how much money we have? Do you have all the inheritance yet?'

He ignored the persistence of her question. He had no intention of giving her control, or even knowledge, of his money. 'I got to go talk to the hay crew.'

'You really need to have a foreman, Lang. Especially if you're going to be gone like that, for a week or two at a time, sometimes.'

Lang nodded. 'I 'spect that'd be a good idee, anyhow. I been thinkin' Cole'd make a good fore-man.'

He hurried off. More and more he was uncomfortable with the whole thing. He had bought into Freda's dream of being a big rancher, but he knew he wasn't capable of managing a big ranch. That meant Freda would have to do much of the managing.

Freda's idea of managing was to spend lots and lots of money. Even the surprisingly large amount from the bank robbery in Cheyenne was proving too little for the scope of her ambitions. And he was too far into the plans to back down on them now. He had to have another infusion of cash. He just had no idea where to turn.

'Hey, Mr Hart! Haf you got a minute?'

He turned to see Virgil Olson waving at him. 'It's lookin' mighty fine,' he greeted the carpenter.

'Yah,' Virgil agreed. 'It is coming along very nicely, I tank. Fine barn. Der bunkhouse and der cook-house, too. We vill be done in maybe tree more veeks. You vill have enough money for dat I can pay my mens, den, yah?'

'Sure,' Lang responded, trying not to look or sound worried. 'Do you know how much it's gonna come to, yet?'

'Well, yah, I tank I haf it figured pretty close. I tank, for all tree buildings ve haf built vill be tree tousands fife hundred dollars.'

'Three thousand five hundred.'

'Yah. I tought maybe I should say someting now. I tought maybe you vould haf to go to der bank for so much money, so you vould need time for doing dat. I tank you probably do not keep all your money hid on der place like Clarence Mobley.'

'Clarence Mobley? I don't guess I know him.'

'Oh, he is dat bachelor fella dat lifs over on Spring Crick. He has dat homestead right vere der liddle waterfall comes down in der pool at der head of dat valley.'

'Oh, yeah. I've seen it. Talked to him once, I guess. Not much of a place, though.'

'No, he does not spend no money. But dey say he hafs an awful lot of it. It is said of him dat he vas a very rich man, vat lost der voman he vanted to marry to somc otter man. So he comed out here and made a homestead and lifs alone and does not much talk to anybody. He yust sits der on all dat money and pines for his lost love. It is a very sad story, yah?'

Lang's voice was distant. 'Doesn't trust banks, huh?'

'Oh, no, by golly. He does not go near to a bank. Der man what stole der voman he lofed, he vas a banker. Somebody told me dat she tought der banker had lots of money, and Clarence, he did not haf no money, so she chose der banker. And der banker is so tight mit his money he does not let her haf even a decent stove. She has to prop the door of her oven shut mit a stick, because for it is broken, and her husband vill not pay to haf it fixed. And Clarence vould haf let her spend all his money, if she had not chose der wrong man. It is too funny, yah?'

'Can you beat thet,' Lang marveled. 'So he just sits there on all thet money, an' her livin' like a pauper, married to a banker.'

'It is too funny, yah?' Virgil repeated. 'So dat is vy he vill haf notting to do vith banks, I tank. But I vorry for him sometimes.'

'Why's thet?'

'Well, dey haf told me dat sometimes ven he gets lonesome, and somebody comes along to talk vith him, he vill drink too much.'

'Likes his whiskey, huh?'

'Yah, sometimes. Und ven he drinks too much of it, he talks about how much of der money his voman could haf had, if she had chosen him instead of der banker. Und sometimes, dey tell me, he vill show dem vere he has hidden der money, und show dem how much of it der is. I vorry about dat. Sometime he vill show dat to der wrong man.'

'That's sure likely to happen, all right enough,' Lang agreed.

'Vell, I haf to get back to keep mine crew vorking. You vill haf der tree tousands fife hundred dollars for me in tree veeks?'

Lang nodded. 'I'll have to make a trip to Casper to get it out of the bank. I ain't like Clarence. I ain't about ta keep thet kinda money layin' about.'

'I tank dat is much der smarter,' Virgil agreed as he headed back to work.

'Now wouldn't that jist be somethin',' Lang mused as he walked back to the house.

As he approached the house, Freda's scream froze him in his tracks. She screamed again, and the scream was cut short. He sprinted toward the house and burst in through the front door.

Two men he had never seen stood in his front room. One of them was looking on and laughing, as the other ripped the clothes from Freda. As he burst in, they both whirled to face him. He stopped cold in his tracks.

The man who was tearing at Freda's clothes stepped away from her. His hand dropped to just above the well-worn butt of the Colt .45 tied low on his hip. The other man did the same, the smile never leaving his face.

Sweat erupted from Lang's forehead. He looked back and forth, from one man to the other. The eyes of both men were cold, expressionless. He knew they were killers, and he could not hope to match both of them. His knees began to tremble.

'You best walk outa here, little man,' one of the men said quietly. 'You ain't gonna be no help to the little lady, especially when you're dead.'

Lang's eyes darted from one man to the other. Then he looked at Freda. She stood leaning against the wall. A large bruise marred the side of her beautiful face. Blood trickled from the corner of her mouth. She held her torn dress up in front of her in a vain effort to cover herself. Panic held her eyes wide, staring.

A lifetime of cowardice that he loathed suddenly drained from Hart's being. He felt it wash down him, starting from his head, to drain into the floor beneath him. In its place a rising tide of anger rose up and swelled within him.

Without thinking, he whipped his gun from its holster with a speed he had never known, thumbing the hammer as it rose. It sent a deafening roar into the confines of the front room as it levelled on the chest of the nearest would-be rapist.

With no hesitation he swung the gun to the second man, thumbing the hammer as he moved. · The man's own gun was already clear of the holster, lifting toward him. He felt no fear. A cold core of ice gripped his stomach instead of the cramps he had felt so often. He fired. The bullet struck the gunman less than a heartbeat before his own gun barked. It was enough. The impact of Lang's bullet jarred him enough for his shot to go wide of the mark. He dropped the gun and collapsed on to the floor.

Lang swung his gun back to the first gunman. He lay where he had fallen, unmoving. Lang looked back at the second gunman. No movement stirred the silent form. Then he looked at his wife.

Freda stood against the wall, frozen in fear. Her eyes stared wildly into the eyes of her husband. He holstered his gun and reached for her, walking swiftly across the floor. She lunged into his arms, sobbing, clinging to him.

With a sudden burst of exhilaration, Lang realized his pants were dry. Bone dry.

20
When Cowardice Dies

Y.A. Oliver rode at a ground-eating lope. He chewed the corners of his great handlebar moustache nervously. As he neared the top of the rise, he slowed his horse. He removed his hat. As he approached the crest of the ridge, he stopped his horse. Standing in his stirrups, he could just see the crude homestead in the valley below him.

Less than a quarter of a mile behind the shack, a small stream of water cascaded over a high cliff. From this distance, he could not even hear the sound of it plunging into the deep pool at its base. It looked like some silently majestic scene that imparted peace to all who saw it, just by its breathtaking beauty.

Nearer to where the lawman sat his horse, the scene contrasted almost violently with the scenic beauty of the background. A squalid shack, with only a buffalo hide for a door, sat in the middle of half an acre of clutter. Empty bottles and cans, trash of every description, and even a discarded saddle lay strewn about. A crooked stove pipe jutted out of the shack, sagging precariously as though it, too, sought a place amid the clutter to lie down.

A saddled horse was tied to a fence post near the corner of the house. Aside from its impatient stamping and tossing of its head, there was no movement.

The marshal grunted. He lifted his reins and rode over the top of the rise toward the house. 'Looks like maybe I'm in time,' he muttered.

Just then Lang Hart emerged from the house. Oliver swore under his breath and pulled his horse to a stop. Lang glanced up and saw him, sitting his horse, watching. Without hesitation, Lang mounted his horse and rode directly toward the marshal.

Two guns jutted from scabbards on the marshal's saddle. On the left side, ahead of the stirrup and tilted forward, the stock of a Winchester '73 showed. On the right side, behind the stirrup and tilted back, the stock of a double-barrelled shotgun was visible. Y.A. Oliver slipped the short-barrelled, double-barrelled shotgun out of a saddle scabbard, and waited for the approaching rancher.

'You lookin' fer me, Marshal?' Lang asked.

'I'm afraid I am,' the marshal confirmed. 'You best unbuckle your gun and put your hands up, Hart. You are under arrest for half a dozen murders and robberies.'

Lang sighed deeply. 'How'd you figger it out?'

'I just checked with the bank. There was no inheritance sent from South Carolina. You made all the deposits. You made every deposit two days after there was a robbery. In every robbery but one, the folks that were robbed were shot in the back. You robbed the La Bonte stage, and killed the driver, the guard, and the passenger. You didn't get any money from the stage, but Prestamer's family said he was carrying pertneart twelve hundred dollars. Two days later, you deposited eleven hundred dollars in the bank in Casper.

'Somebody robbed the Three Mile Hog ranch down by Fort Fetterman. Nobody knows how much money was took, but two days later you deposited almost fifteen hundred dollars in the bank in Casper.

'Then a storekeeper in Kaycee was gunned down. Shot in the back, again. His daughter said he had five thousand dollars a man had just paid him for the store. He was selling out, going back East. The next day, you paid four thousand dollars cash for a herd of cows. You didn't happen to know what that store-keeper's name was, did you?'

'How would I know thet?'

'Just wondered. His name was Jedediah Doop.'

'Thet don't mean nothin' ta me.'

'It should. When I went out to your place to investigate those two fellas you killed, I visited with your wife some. She told me what a brave war hero you were. She said you'd been awarded the Silver Cross for bravery by Jefferson Davis himself. Showed me the medal, to prove it.'

'I never even showed that to her.'

'No, I don't suppose you did. Especially since it wasn't yours.'

'Whatd'ya mean?'

'In that fancy velvet box it was in, under the part that held the medal, was a piece of that parchment kind of paper they put special awards on. It said the Silver Cross was awarded to Jedediah Doop, by the Confederate Army of America.'

Lang's face drained of color, but he said nothing. The marshal continued, talking faster. 'But I'm gettin' ahead of myself. Then you went to Cheyenne and bought a whole wagonload of haying equipment. Just by coincidence, the bank was robbed while you were there. The bank president and teller weren't shot in the back, though. And about that, I'm surprised. But more than eight thousand dollars was stolen. Their description of their assailant fits you to a T. Two days later you deposited almost eight thousand dollars in the bank in Casper. That's too many coincidences, Hart. You are known to be a coward. Your cowardice has left a trail of carnage half-way across Wyoming, but it's all over. There's one thing I don't understand, though.'

'What's that?'

'Well, up to the time you braced them two hard-cases that attacked your wife, I had you figured for a complete coward. You broke your pattern when you didn't kill the two in the bank at Cheyenne. Then, the other day, standing up to that pair at your ranch was as brave an act as I've seen. I thought maybe you'd changed. Then Virgil told me maybe you was headed out here. I don't know what I'm going to find in old Clarence's place.'

Lang chuckled unexpectedly. 'He's fine, Marshal. Drunk an' passed out, but he ain't hurt. I put all 'is

money what he was a-showin' me back where he had
it, an' put the floorboards over it agin.'

Marshal Ofiver shook his head. 'That doesn't
figure, Hart. What's going on?'

Lang sighed deeply. Instead of answering, he said,
'Freda'll figger I kilt Ralph, won't she?'

The marshal nodded. 'Got to come out. You was
seen practisin' throwin' rocks at that mule, to make
him kick.'

Lang nodded, surprised that he felt none of the
fear that had dogged him all his life. He shook his
head. 'That's the funny part, Marshal. I didn't do it.
I set it up, all right. Jist like the coward I allays been.
Then I couldn't do it. Ralph, he was my friend. But
jist when I decided I couldn't do it, the mule went an'
kicked all by hisself. Jist try an' figger that one out.'

The marshal interrupted his reflection. 'You wanta
tell me what's goin' on?' he asked again.

Lang sighed yet again. 'Ain't much ta tell,
Marshal,' he said. 'You're plumb right 'bout me bein'
a coward. Allays was. An' you're plumb right thet me
bein' a coward left . . . what was thet ya called it? . . .
a trail a carnage? It's a plumb awful trail, I kin tell ya.
I started seein' thet trail in my sleep, pertneart ever'
night. Got plumb tired o' bein' ashamed o' who an'
what I am. I jist got plumb tired o' bein' a coward. I
got tired o' seein' all them faces in the night. I got
tired o' rememberin' how I wet my pants ever' time I
got skeert. I got tired o' bein' 'shamed to see myself
in the mirror ever' time I shaved. I got tired o' killin'
folks. I didn't know, till it was too late ta git rid of 'em,
but ever' man ya kill stays with ya the rest o' your life.

They's all there, starin' at ya, all the time. Cain't even close yer eyes to shut 'em away. Cain't git drunk enough to fergit 'em.'

'That's always the way, if you kill like a coward,' the marshal agreed. 'But not the ones you face like a man, for the right reasons.'

Lang continued as if he hadn't been interrupted. 'There in Cheyenne, I jist couldn't do it. I jist couldn't kill no more. Not like that, anyways. So I busted 'em on the head instead. Then when them two fellers suprised me, a tryin' ta rape Freda, right there in the house, with the carpenters a-workin' down on the barn, I finally found out how ta plumb quit bein' afraid. It didn't matter no more, but I quit bein' afraid. Without her, I didn't have nothin' left ta live fer nohow. If I didn't defend 'er, or die tryin', she'd hate me, an' that'd be worse'n dyin'. So I jist did what a man had oughta do. Sure wish I'da learnt thet twenty years ago.'

'But you still came out here to kill and rob Clarence, after you got him drunk enough to show you where he keeps his money hidden,' the marshal accused.

Lang nodded. 'I did that,' he confessed. 'But I couldn't do that neither. I jist plumb got done bein' a coward an' a thief, an' done asked God ta forgive me. I ended up askin' 'im, could I borry a bunch o' thet money o' his ta tide me through till calf-sellin' time. He said he'd borry it to me, but then 'e went an' passed out afore he could write up an IOU. I figgered I'd come back when he was sober an' try agin.'

'And if he wouldn't do it when he was sober?'

Lang shrugged. 'Try the bank, I 'pect. Don't matter none now, nohow. I 'spect Freda'll lose the place.'

The marshal nodded. 'Most likely. Once you've made a confession of where and when you stole the money, it'll have to go back.'

'And if I don't?'

The marshal shrugged. 'Hard to say, then. Someone may take legal action to try to retrieve the money, but then they'd have to prove it was their money. That might be hard to do.'

'What are you gonna do with me?'

'Hang you, I would expect,' the marshal said matter-of-factly. 'That's usually what we do with folks that shoot people in the back. Now you better shuck that gun.'

'I sure deserve hangin', all right enough, but I cain't face thet,' Lang asserted. 'I seen a man hung once. His face turned all blue. His tongue come out one corner of 'is mouth. He kicked an' squirmed, an' suffered somethin' awful.'

'If you don't get your hand off that gun, you ain't gonna have the chance to find out,' the marshal said. 'Now unbuckle it and let it drop.'

Lang looked at the twin bores of the shotgun centered on his chest. He saw the calm determination in the marshal's face. He saw, in his mind, the face of the man he had watched hanged.

With a sudden chuckle, he said, 'I guess the best thing I kin leave Freda is jist to not confess nothin', then.'

He jerked his pistol free of its holster. It was just lifting to point toward the marshal when a load of buckshot tore into his chest. He flew backward out of the saddle. He landed heavily on the ground. His horse pranced away, snorting. He smiled slightly. Funny, he thought, learnt courage jist in time to die without wettin' my pants.

'Well, at least you died a brave man,' the marshal muttered. 'I 'spect maybe that counts for something.'

Maybe it does.